Sandra Birdsell

Sandra Birdsell was born in Morris, Manitoba, a small town south of Winnipeg. In the mid sixties, she moved with her family to Winnipeg, and began writing several years later as her children grew up. Since then, her stories have been published in anthologies and journals such as *Grain, NeWest Review*, and *Capilano*. *Night Travellers* is Ms. Birdsell's first book. A founding member of the Manitoba Writers Guild, Ms. Birdsell currently lives in Winnipeg.

Mary Pratt

Mary Pratt was born in 1935 in Fredericton, New Brunswick. She studied at the University of New Brunswick and at Mount Allison University, School of Fine Arts, where she received her degree in 1961. Her work has been shown in many exhibitions in private and public galleries in Canada and abroad, including the National Gallery of Canada and the London Regional Art Gallery, which organized and circulated a fourteen-year-survey exhibition in 1981-82.

New Press Canadian Classics

Distinguished by the use of Canadian fine art on its covers, New Press Canadian Classics is an innovative, much-needed series of high-quality, reasonably priced editions of the very best Canadian fiction, nonfiction and poetry.

New Press Canadian Classics

new press CANADIAN CLASSICS

Sandra Birdsell

Night Travellers

General Publishing Co. Limited
Toronto, Canada

Turnstone Press edition
published in 1982

General Paperback edition
published in 1984

ISBN 0-7736-7173-0

Printed and bound in Canada

for Roger, Angela and Darcie

These stories have previously appeared in the following
publications:

"Flowers for Weddings and Funerals" in *NeWest Review*
and in *Manitoba Stories*, Queenston House

"The Wednesday Circle" in *Grain*

"The Wild Plum Tree" in *NeWest Review*

"Stones" in *Capilano Review*

The author wishes to thank the Manitoba Arts Council
for a grant which aided in the writing of this book.

CONTENTS

The Flood

MAURICE Lafrenier stood on the fire escape on the south side of the hotel and looked with awe at the litter-strewn lake which spread out where the town had been only two weeks ago.

"My God," he said, because he needed to hear the sound of his own voice. He felt abandoned, as though he were the only remaining human on earth.

Across the street, a chunk of dirt-riddled ice battered against the Bank of Montreal. The wind had swept the ice into town during the night. He'd lain shivering in bed, warding off the dampness with the glowing rings of his hotplate and listening to that ice crashing like a battering ram against everything that was his. And his thoughts had run together, had overflowed: his submerged business, the barber chairs bolted to the floor, one hundred years old, at least. Brought up from St. Paul on a steamboat, bequeathed to him by Henry Roy who had been like a father to him and who had also taught him his barbering trade. Mika, in Choritza, awaiting the birth of their sixth child. His other five children, cut off, wood chips floating about until the flood would subside. And his mother. When exhaustion had overcome the noise of the ice, he'd dreamt of his mother who was not dead, but alive in his dream, standing beside the river. She was gathering willow branches for her baskets. She'd looked up suddenly and she was not as he'd remembered, defeated and broken, eyes turned inward. But her broad face was strong and serious, her black eyes demanding his attention. If you have a large family, she said, you will need a bigger boat.

He thought of his boat moored below and smiled. They didn't come any smaller than his rowboat. He pulled his tweed cap tighter on his head and made his way carefully down the ice-coated fire escape. One slip and he'd be gone. Two minutes was all a person could hope for in the icy water even if he could get the hipwaders off. And then the little woman would be a widow, his children fatherless. The town would rush in for a woman like Mika. The town thought Mika had taken him in hand and with her clean habits and Mennonite ways had made him what he was today.

His boat rose and fell with the waves, its wood squeaking and protesting against the piece of wooden sidewalk he'd lashed to the bottom of the fire escape to serve as a dock. Water, as far as the eye could see. Who would have thought that their tired, narrow river could have come to this? He told himself that he was anxious to see how the men at the courthouse had endured the ice. Damned fools, he called them, for letting a few rats in the hotel frighten them from sleeping safely as he did. But he knew his real anxiety. It had surfaced during the night and he needed to reassure himself that this flood had happened gradually, others knew about it too. It was not something that had happened overnight to him alone. He was not the only human being left in the world.

He crouched, moved low in the boat and seated himself in the centre of it. No one accused him of being a careless person anymore. He still took chances, certainly, but not until he was sure everything was shipshape first. He untied the knot which moored his boat to the fire escape. He pushed off from the sidewalk with the oar and sliced deeply through the ice slush floating on the surface as he headed out toward the centre of Main Street. He wondered what condition the courthouse basement would be in. It was not what you'd call shipshape. No matter what Bill Livingston said, he would try and persuade the others to move into the hotel before it was too late.

Up and down the wide street, there wasn't another boat to be seen, no human sounds, just the wind and water rushing against the buildings. He stopped rowing, let the oars sink deep into the water and stared for a moment at the bottom of the boat where his boots had crushed through the film of muddy ice. He felt the oar scrape against one of the drowned vehicles that had been parked on Main Street and he shuddered. It was like disturbing the dead, bumping into submerged things. He began rowing against the current which swept down from the mouth of the Agassiz River, across the cemetery and into town. The bottom of the hotel sign bobbed in the water. The sign had been sheared off by the ice during the night, one of the sounds that had kept him awake. He'd been kept awake all spring by the sounds of the ice cracking and groaning like a woman about to give birth. What are you up to, he'd asked the river. Gather up your skirts, it's time, he said, fancying the sound of his thoughts, the idea that the river was a pregnant woman. But its deep complaining rumble made him uneasy. Then, when the weather turned on them, becoming bitterly cold with freezing rain and snowstorms, he sent his children away and only he and Mika remained. They'd been

prepared. The flood hadn't taken him by surprise. The last
of the townspeople had been evacuated only three days ago,
taken like cattle in boats with the few things they had time to
pack and loaded onto railcars at the CN line. Evacuees, flood
victims, the *Free Press* called them.

Agassiz evacuation climaxes grim saga, the headline read.
The saga of the rivers. The Agassiz and the Red meeting head-
long in the north end of town, each carrying full loads into the
late-melting tributaries. The pincer-like movement caused the
waters near the mouth of the Agassiz to back up in twenty-four
hours and run across Main Street at Agassiz Bridge. The saga
of the government engineer's stupidity: "We expect nothing
this year to approach the '48 flood."

"Expect?" Maurice had said and smacked the report in the
newspaper with the back of his hand. "How can anyone expect
things from the river? You listen and watch and you can feel
what's going to happen. You don't go by charts and expect.
It's unpredictable."

The barbershop had become the meeting place for the
daily discussions about the possibilities of the river's flooding.
Maurice, standing at the barber chair cutting hair, had remained
silent until now. He was surprised by his outburst, to find
himself throwing aside the need to be agreeable and to keep
the peace with all around him at any cost. But if he knew
anything well, it was the river. The knowledge was hidden
inside him and flowed out naturally when he put his mind
to it. The conversation which had centred around Bill Livingston, Agassiz's mayor, trailed away. The men stared at Maurice.

He was standing on an edge. His word on the line. "I'm
telling you. If you know what's good for you, then get ready
for a doozer of a flood."

In the same tone of voice Bill Livingston had used thirty
odd years ago when he'd pulled the blanket up over Maurice's
mother's face and said to those present, "Now that's drunk.

Dead drunk. But what can you expect?" he got up from the bench, walked over to the barber chair and stuck his red face into Maurice's. "Horse shit," he said. "You'll have everyone running for the hills."

Maurice caught sight of his own reflection in the mirror above the bench where the men had gathered. He moved around the chair gracefully, he was light on his feet. He wore his thick black hair swept back, it made him look taller. He saw the slender back of himself, the blue birthmark on his neck, while in the plate glass mirror above his marble sinks, he could see the front of himself. Mika fed him well. He had the beginning of a double chin and a slight paunch. He saw himself begin to gesture expansively, his hand extended, palm up in a sweeping motion. Look here, he was going to say to Livingston, I'm an agreeable man. He dropped his arm quickly.

"Use your head. Forget what they're saying in Winnipeg. Those dumbells can't forecast a flood until they're up to their asses in water. I predict that it'll be the worst flood ever."

Maurice's breath came faster now as he rowed against a small side current where the water swept between two buildings. He'd said it. His word had stood and one by one the men had begun to trust his knowledge and come to him for advice. He passed by the barbershop. He passed by the movie theatre. The sign on the marquee, THE LADY TAKES A SAILOR, used to make him laugh, but because of the ferocity of the flood, now seemed to him to have been a portent filled with meaning.

Freed of the metal graveyard of drowned vehicles that had been parked down Main Street, Maurice stopped rowing. He started up the small outboard motor that Flood Control had issued him. Engine straining, he moved out faster into the current, the bow whacking against the choppy water. And then he saw the lights of the courthouse beaming out at him from the tall narrow windows. So, the basement, she'd held. The courthouse had been built up on its foundation. It was entrenched behind sandbags, but water lapped inches from the top of the dike. He heard the sound of another motor and tension fled from his muscles. He wasn't alone. A boat moved out from behind the courthouse, its hull cutting a deep V down into the water. It veered suddenly in his direction. He shut down his motor and waited. There were three men in the boat, two of them farmers from the area, and Woods, a young RCMP officer whose cap appeared to be held in place by his ears.

"What's up?" Maurice asked.

Stevens, the younger one of the farmers, motioned wearily to the west. All three men looked alike, unshaven, complexions grey from too much coffee and too little sleep. Maurice saw the rifles on the floor of their boat.

"He's got fifty head of Herefords," Woods said. His voice rose to an excited screech. "They're stranded. Haven't been able to get feed into them. Not sure they'll even be there now, not after this ice."

"That was some night," Maurice said. "Have you checked the basement?"

"It's tighter than a drum," Woods said, echoing a Livingston pronouncement.

That was the whole damned trouble. It was too tight. There was too much pressure on the walls. They should flood the basement or the whole thing would pop inward. Damned farmers. The closest they'd been to water before the flood was the dugouts they'd led their cows down to and Woods was still wet behind his big flapping ears.

"What's the situation with the livestock?" he asked.

Stevens lifted one of the rifles and laid it across his knees.

"Plain damned shame. Something should be done," Maurice said. He'd told Stevens, ship 'em out. If you don't, may as well shoot them now. "We're all in the same condition," he said. "My shop, your cattle. We'll have to start over, that's all." He was surprised by his own sudden optimism.

It was what Henry Roy would have said. He'd dispensed good will like pills when the going got tough.

"Sure we will," the farmer said. "With what? The money I'll get from this year's crop?"

"Something's bound to come up," Maurice said. "Wait and see, the government will come through in the end."

The farmer spat. "Laurent doesn't even know where Agassiz is," he said. "And all they care about on Broadway is making sure the houses on Wellington Crescent don't get wet."

"Watch, watch," Maurice called out suddenly as a sharp piece of ice swept close to their boats. He angled his craft away into the waves. The ice slid inches from the hull of the other boat and then was gone. The three men watched it pass by. Maurice could tell they were unaware of the danger. It was a wonder there hadn't been a serious accident, what with the mayor heading up the flood control committee. He had a bulldozer for a brain. Ran over people who didn't agree with him. Sent people running off half-cocked to do what they damned well should have done a month ago.

"If that one had hit, you'd have been able to drive a grain truck through the hole," Maurice said. He felt strong, in control. "Keep your eyes open out there. An aluminium boat is no damned good in this stuff." Old Man River. That was the name they'd given to him since his prediction of the flood had come true. Maurice Lafreniere reads the river like it was a newspaper. When the going gets tough, the tough gets going, he told himself. And he'd proven himself. Why do you have to stay, now of all times, Mika had asked. And he couldn't explain to her that for once he didn't want to be on the outside, left out, but dead centre. Because Mika didn't know otherwise. He was the one who went out each morning to check the waters' rising, measured on a pole at Agassiz Bridge, and took the reading to the courthouse where the police radioed it into Winnipeg.

"Why don't you come with us?" Woods asked.

Hold your hand, you mean. "I'm going to take the reading and then cruise around a bit, see what damage I can do. Was there any breakfast? Could eat a horse."

"We'll bring you one," Stevens said.

Maurice chuckled at the bad joke. His spirits rose. He watched the three men head out across the open field. It was just a case of numbers to Ottawa: 28:1. If they could get the real story. Drop Laurent down in the middle of this hell, get his feet wet and he wouldn't say, "No aid for the flood victims."

He tied the boat to the railing on the bridge. He didn't dare venture into the river channel, it was choked with debris. He took the binoculars from beneath the seat and lifted them. The water rose and fell at the level of 29:3 on the pole. He predicted that the crest was days away. Three more feet of water and even the tops of the trees, the only remaining indication of where the river's bank used to be, would be under. They were like scrawny black fingers now, pointing out the sweep and curve of the shoreline where he'd spent that terrible summer hiding from the priest who would take him to be with his brothers in the convent in the city. The memory caught at him suddenly like a camouflaged barb hooking an unsuspecting fish.

He turned the glasses toward the cemetery. His hands shook with the cold. All the grave stones had vanished, had been tumbled by the waves or cut down by the ice and scattered like broken teeth at the bottom of the lake. He lowered the glasses. His eyes stung. His mother and father were there. They were side by side, locked into their early middle years behind the frozen ground. First his father; a railroad accident. And there had been no town clamouring to rescue that widow. She'd been ignored. Left alone to feed three kids with the money she made sewing and from her baskets. And a month later, they buried her. Dead drunk. Lying on her back in the centre of the bed, her head in a pool of grey vomit. Perspiration ran down between his shoulder blades.

Hey, boy, do you want to keep these, Livingston had asked, holding up his mother's beaded moccasins. He'd come with a number of other men, now forgotten, to help carry her away and to poke around through the remains of his family. The wind rose and the icy blast of it seemed to bore straight through his skull. He wished suddenly that he'd been able to find one place for his children instead of shipping them off, piece by piece, to live out the flood among strangers. The ice slush was like crushed glass as it slid swiftly beneath and around his boat. He rowed steadily. His arms began to ache. The sound of a shrill whistle jarred him. He turned quickly and saw the huge white hull of a fishing vessel bearing down on him. It was the *Apex*, bringing supplies to Agassiz.

They plucked Maurice from his rowboat and towed his boat back to town. They took him back to the courthouse, unloaded the supplies, had something to eat, and then Maurice, by virtue of his title, Old Man River, was invited to come along on a cruise about the town to show a newspaper reporter who had come to see for himself what damage had been done.

"This is incredible," the man said. His name was Charles Medlake. The tall thin man spoke to them as though they hadn't already known that the flood was incredible, devastating, all the fancy words he used to describe what had happened to their town. "I've never seen anything like this," he kept saying.

He thinks he pays us a compliment, Maurice thought. Being ten feet under is a great accomplishment. He stood at the railing on the stern of the *Apex* with Bill Livingston and the reporter, listening to their conversation with growing impatience.

"I bloody well hope that we never do again, either," said Bill Livingston, but there was a strange tone of pride in his booming voice. "But according to an Indian legend, this happens every hundred years."

Medlake's hands shook as he cupped them and lit another cigarette. He drew deeply on it and expelled shreds of blue smoke which were snatched by the wind. "Have many people left the area for good?" he asked.

"Hell no. We're tough chickens."

Maurice shifted from one foot to another as the reporter asked the mayor many questions. According to an Indian legend? That was the first he'd heard of it. What Indian? Outwardly, he appeared solid and calm. His parka was unzipped, revealing his green curling sweater with the white rearing bucks on it. Mika's mother had knit it for him. He chewed thoughtfully on a toothpick, moving it from one side of his mouth to the other.

"This isn't the worst of it," the mayor said. "We haven't been east of town yet. The ice took out three or four houses."

"I've seen enough for now," the man said. He flicked his half-smoked cigarette over the stern. "Listen, the luckiest house in Agassiz is the worst hit in Winnipeg. I never saw anything this bad in the city."

"Really?" the mayor said.

It was what Maurice had suspected. Once they'd figured it out, that the same river that was flooding Agassiz would eventually flood Winnipeg, they screamed bloody murder. Squeaky wheel gets the grease.

"I'd like to get back to the courthouse and call the paper to send out a photographer. This should be recorded."

Livingston called out directions to the pilot. The fishing boat began a slow wide turn.

"The feds have got to open their eyes to this," Livingston said. "Pictures would help. We estimate that property damage alone will be close to five million dollars. Then there's the months of lost revenue to consider." He turned suddenly to Maurice. "How long has it been since you've earned a cent, Maurie?"

"Eh?" He was jolted loose from his tumbling thoughts.

"I said, how are you going to manage to feed the kiddies when they get home? Let alone afford the lumber to rebuild the house and buy new furniture?"

"Well, I...," Maurice began and stopped. I was prepared. My furniture is high and dry. We took what was left of the preserves to Mika's sister's place. But there was something in Livingston's tone of voice that kept him quiet. He sensed that there was more here than an innocent question.

Livingston didn't wait for his reply. "We must be compensated. We're going to need money and lots of it. Interest-free money for the business community to replace their inventory. I've lost my entire stock of hardware. The farmers, their seed and fertilizer. And people like Maurie, here, they'll need money to feed and clothe the family. He's got six kids."

"Five," Maurice said. "I've got five." He was stung. Money for people like Maurie, here. How are you going to feed your family? A straightforward question. But it rankled. It was intended to remind him that at one time he'd swept their floors, carried out their shit pails and shovelled clean the barns. He'd fallen down drunk in the street. He'd been looked upon with pity or scorn. And that he had risen only so far in twenty years that his main concern would be how to feed six mouths, nothing more. He sees me as being another flood victim, same as all the others. Maurice freed his hands from his parka pockets and cut the air in front of the two men in an impatient motion.

"Compensation, to be sure," he said.

"What was that?" Charles Medlake spoke directly to him for the first time.

"Compensation, to be sure. By all means." His was the quiet reasonable voice of Henry Roy, his mentor. He hoped it was the voice of someone who would listen for so long to the clamour of others and then, with a few chosen words, bring clarity to their ramblings so as to make them look ridiculous. "But look here, compensation and interest-free loans are only a small part of the whole picture," he continued.

The newsman moved in closer. He began to make notes on a tablet. "Just what do you think should be done?"

"Many things. Certainly, I could use a hand just as everyone else in this town could use a hand. I'm a business man too. I've lost more than furniture." He avoided Livingston's eyes. "But I personally wouldn't care if I didn't get a penny from the government if we could take steps to make certain that this here flood will never happen again."

Livingston laughed outright and turned away.

"But how is that possible?" Medlake asked.

Maurice was unsettled by the laughter. He shoved his hands back into his pockets. They were heading back toward the courthouse. They had circled the town and approached the stone building from behind, moving slowly down Elm Avenue. The trees were bare, bark black with orange rusty-looking growths in the crooks of limbs. A chair was caught in the lower branches of one tree. Maurice cleared his throat to speak. Build a sewage treatment plant so we no longer shit and piss on the river. We didn't have floods like this one until we got the running water. My God, the river, she doesn't pretend to be beautiful, but some honour is due, eh? Lure the goldeye and pickerel back with clean water. Forget the Indian legend that says we have no say in the matter. We should remember the river. She gave this region its life. But he knew they saw the river with different eyes. To them it was heavy, sluggish and ugly, a breeding ground for mosquitoes and eels.

"It's impossible to prevent flooding," Livingston said. He took Medlake by the elbow and attempted to steer him away by pointing out some particular damage.

"Wait, let him finish," Medlake said.

"We need to look to the future," Maurice said.

"How?"

"With all our minds, we should be able to come up with something instead of just saying it happens every hundred years. We should think about building a permanent dike around the town, for instance, or dig drainage ditches in the country to let the spring run-off enter into the Red further downstream."

"Winnipeg would never go for that," Livingston interrupted. "Because it would mean more water for them."

He speaks as though he has just bit into a lemon, Maurice thought.

"There must be a way around it," Medlake said.

The boat nudged slowly into the courthouse yard toward a large oak tree in the centre of it. The pilot cut the engine and Maurice was jolted forward as the craft met bark with a hollow thud. The *Apex* whistled its arrival. Dark shapes appeared at the window and then the back door swung open. Woods and Stevens stepped out on the stairs. They climbed into Maurice's rowboat and began rowing toward them. Woods cupped his hands to his mouth. "Survivors," he shouted. "We found two women and a child stranded on the roof of a granary."

"Listen," Medlake said to Maurice. "I'd like to talk to you later on. What you say makes good sense."

Maurice felt the careful attentive posture of Livingston's large body. "Suits me," he said, trying to sound casual.

"Where can I find you?"

"If I'm not here—"

"He's over at the hotel," the mayor finished. "Maurie here doesn't like our company. He's always been what you might call a lone wolf."

Maurice's face grew warm. "Shoot, it's not that," he said. He felt as though his mouth was full of marbles. He juggled words in his mind. "It's not that. It's the basement. She's going to cave in."

"What?" Medlake asked. "And you're taking me in there?"

"He doesn't know what he's talking about," Livingston said. "The walls are two feet thick. This place is built like a brick shithouse."

The rowboat came alongside and they got into it. Maurice sat between the two men, slouched down into his parka, his fists curled tightly inside his pockets. Blow, goddammit, he urged as they approached the courthouse. Now. He imagined walls crumbling.

They removed their hipwaders in the basement. Maurice sat on the cot in the jail cell and leaned against the rough Tyndalstone wall and closed his eyes.

"Well, Maurie," Livingston said and laughed. "Drainage ditches, eh? It looks as though the wrong one ran for mayor."

Maurice didn't answer. He could see his parents' fresh graves, a mixture of yellow clay and top-soil. This room carried the memory. The priest had found him beside the river, trying to build a raft so that he could float downstream to his mother's people. And had agreed, Maurice could stay. He didn't have to join his brothers in the convent in the city. He'd sat in this very cell, tracing the outlines of strange creatures locked in the stone without knowing what they were while the men of the town decided his fate. Send for his mother's people, the priest advised. And so he waited it out in this room for a full week. They didn't want me, he asked. Henry Roy winked. You wouldn't have wanted them, he said. I never sent the message. And he took Maurice in and gave him work in the hotel. It would have turned out well if it hadn't been that it took too long for a town to forget a person who would die suffocating on their own vomit. Dead drunk.

"Come on, Old Man River," Livingston said and clapped him on the shoulder. "Let's go on up and meet those survivors."

Maurice followed him into the main hall. Two women and the child huddled beneath blankets within the circle of men. The men parted to let Maurice and Livingston through. The women and child were of mixed blood, Maurice realized instantly. Mongrels. The women had identical expressions, wide smiles, like fools, displaying their rotting teeth. Don't let anyone tell you different, Henry Roy had said, mongrels don't make better dogs. But the child studied Maurice with the same serious black eyes as his mother had in his dream last night. If you're going to have a large family, she said, you will need a bigger boat. These people didn't even have a boat. Not even a small one. The men seemed to be waiting for him to do something.

"Do you speak French?" Maurice asked the women.

They laughed and covered the gaping holes in their teeth with hands that looked to be tinged by wood smoke.

Maurice felt the floor move.

"No, no, not French," Livingston said. "You never know. You could be related. Say something to them in Indian."

"In a pig's ass," Maurice said, his anger breaking loose in upraised fists. The floor beneath him tilted. And then there was a sound, like thunder, beneath them. Relief flooded every part of his body and his knees suddenly felt weak. He felt like laughing hysterically.

Stevens ran into the room. "Clear out," he yelled. "The basement just went."

The reporter scrambled for his parka. Maurice led the women and child to the back door. They were calm. They pulled their blankets about themselves and walked slowly, as though they were accustomed to calamities. Bill Livingston ran to the tables, gathered papers to his chest, set them back down again. Maurice heard the roar of the water filling the basement, flooding the little room. He lifted the child quickly and handed her to Stevens. When she saw the boat, she clung to Maurice's sweater and began to cry. He peeled her loose and handed her down. I was right, he told himself. Once again, I was right. He felt like laughing and he felt like crying. Thank God, the *Apex* was big enough, it would hold them all. It would carry the whole damned works of them to the hills.

Boundary Lines

"HOWDY Doody," Maurice said as a customer sat down in his barber chair. The greeting was intended to disarm, one he reserved for strangers. With a flourish, he swept the striped barber cloth around the man's wide shoulders and fastened it with a clip at his sunburned neck.

SCISSORS SHARPENED WHILE YOU WAIT: 25 CENTS.
DRESSMAKERS TAKE NOTE: 3 FOR $1.00!!

His sign, intended as a joke, blared from one corner of the plate glass mirror and above it:

WE NEED YOUR HEAD IN OUR BUSINESS

Head number twenty-nine. And judging from the smell, this head hadn't been washed in a week. Maurice made a note to dip the comb into disinfectant when he'd finished with this one.

"Want me to lower your ears a bit, eh?"

The man laughed, settled back and crossed his legs. His work boots were caked with yellow clay. Maurice recognized him as one of the Franklin brothers the council had hired from a neighbouring municipality to help construct the ring dike around the town. All day, the incessant rumbling of the heavy machinery could be heard as earth around Agassiz was scraped flat in preparation for the dike. In the north end of town, truck-loads of dirt were already being dumped into place.

"She's one hot day," the man said.

"You betcha." Maurice in his crisp white barber shirt, its collar like a priest's collar, appeared to be cool. The high neck and heavily starched shirt would prevent splinters of hair from becoming imbedded in his skin, but it also kept his body heat in. He raised his arms and winced with the pain that shot into his cramped muscles. Along the far wall, sitting on a bench, three men waited their turn. Behind the half-wall partition, all six pooltables were in use and thick smoke curled in the lights above the tables.

Maurice parted the man's sandy-coloured hair, combed it into place. He reached for the scissors. "So, how's the work going on the dike?" he asked. "Everything going according to Hoyle?"

The man's hair was coarse and flew from the tips of his scissors, spraying the front of his shirt. Maurice only half-listened while the man talked, nodding occasionally and saying, "Oh, I see."

The smell of smoke mixed with hair tonic and the heavy odour that came from the pile of multi-coloured hair on the floor made his stomach churn. It had become his smell. It lingered in all of his clothing, in his leather tool kit, so that when he took the kit home with him to cut his children's hair, the smell was there in the house as well. He'd been looking forward to getting away from it, had anticipated the weekend and fishing with his brothers. Now, he didn't know what he'd do. He'd have to telephone them and make up some excuse. He couldn't say, my wife doesn't want you in the house.

"How long since your last haircut?" Maurice asked. He would know from the man's reply, his preference, how much to cut off. Then he listened while the man recited the list of complaints, machinery breakdowns, about the houses that still had to be moved inside the dike's boundaries.

When Maurice had come to work that morning, it had been with Mika's "over my dead body" echoing in his ears. Smoke from forest fires had blown in over the town during the night and hung low, turning the sun red. The effect was like Mika's anger, tinging all with a faint golden hue, making him feel uneasy, strange, as though his feet were not touching the ground completely. "Over your dead body, eh? Well, that could be arranged," he'd retorted. She'd reminded him of his brothers' last visit. How Alphonse had gotten drunk and puked on the kitchen floor. But the worst of it, she said, standing there at the door with her hands on her hips, was that they'd spoken French the whole time.

"Maurice Ovide Lafreniere?" a voice said behind him, sending his thoughts scattering. The voice was low, husky, as though the person had a cold.

"Yes?" Maurice stopped snipping, stood poised with the scissors suspended in mid-air.

"You are the person responsible for the digging?"

Maurice turned slowly to face an old man. "I beg your pardon? I think you confuse me with someone else."

"Are you Maurice Lafreniere?" His face was a ripple of corrugated wrinkles from squinting into the sun and the wind. Mucus, like yellow pearls, had congealed in the corners of his black eyes. He was shorter than Maurice and of slight build. He raised his hand and Maurice saw that it was smooth and strong looking, the cords in his wrist sinewy ropes beneath his brown skin.

"Absolutely," Maurice said. The smell of the man made his eyes burn. It was the same smell that still clung to the corners of the furnace room. It was the sour smell of the flood. Why didn't these people stay on the reservation where they belonged? As long as there were people like Mika who would buy their braided door mats, invite them in for bread and jam, they would continue to come traipsing in looking for handouts.

"And you? I haven't had the pleasure."

"Norbert Desmarais, your uncle," the man said. "You should know who I am."

Maurice dropped the scissors. He bent to retrieve them. Where the man had walked, wet smudges trailed across the clean tile floor. The old man's feet were thickly caked with Red River gumbo and he was splattered to the knees with hardened mud the shape of clams which clung to the wool fabric of his pants. When Maurice stood up, his heart thrashed against his rib cage.

"Well," Maurice said. "Long time, no see. What's bringing you here to Agassiz?"

"The digging," Desmarais said. "I heard you're the person who made the digging happen."

Franklin shifted impatiently beneath the barber cloth. "We're the ones doing the digging. What's it to you?"

Maurice moved slowly, his actions a cover for his confusion. He began cutting hair once again. "If you're speaking of the dike, then it was my idea, to be sure. But it was put before the town and voted on in a fair manner."

"And you know where they're bringing the earth from?"

"Well, I'm not certain, but the municipality owns several—"

"It's yours."

"Mine?"

"They're bringing the earth from Grande Pointe. Land that belonged to your family. Something should be done about it."

Maurice grew aware of the silence in the barbershop. Keen interest was being taken in this conversation. "I've never lived at Grande Pointe," he said quietly. Maurice Lafreniere has a good head, it was often said. He kept everything going straight in this crooked place. He was calm now, and had the situation in control. "I believe my mother's relations once lived in Grande Pointe, but that was years ago."

"Trees," the old man said. He jerked his arm up to the window where cars and trucks parked at an angle against the sidewalk. The glare of the red sun made the windshields look solid, like a sheet of hot metal. A truck engine revved suddenly as another load of heavy earth slid into place on the dike.

"Eh?"

"From here to the river. Trees. Do you remember?"

"Absolutely," Maurice said and laughed. He scanned the bench where the men sat waiting. Above their heads was a sign which read: WORK LIKE HELEN B. HAPPY. In two seconds, he'd ask the man to leave.

"Same as Grande Pointe. Trees, from here to the river. All gone. They cut the trees and haul away the dirt so that they can pile it up around the town of Agassiz."

"Well Uncle, I don't know about any land. But even if what you say is the case, then that was well before my time. There are no records. The land belongs to the municipality now. What can I do?"

The old man jerked away impatiently. "And your tongue? That too was taken away long ago?"

"My tongue is rusty, to be sure. But it's there when I need it."

"Speak to me then," the old man said in French.

Maurice glanced about. "It's not polite," he said.

"When you're in Rome, you do what the Romans do," Franklin said.

"Absolutely." Maurice agreed.

Desmarais ignored the comment. "And your children? What about them? They are also too polite to speak French?"

"There's no need to," Maurice said. "What this gentleman says is true."

"Ah. You think no further than the end of your thick nose. There's no need. There's no need for you to come and take back your land either. You have all this," he said. His black eyes took in the whole room for the first time. He moved in a circle as he looked at everything and his eyes finally rested on the buffalo head on the wall. Maurice had rescued it from behind the curling rink after flood clean-up and had mounted it above the plate glass mirror. He used it to hang his hat on. The old man smiled and then began to laugh. His shoulders shook violently and he leaned against the barber chair to support himself.

The customers' interest in the man had changed to wariness. Maurice sensed it. Desmarais began coughing. His high narrow chest heaved beneath his plaid shirt.

"Calm yourself," Maurice said. He steeled himself against the man's odour and taking him by the elbow, steered him over to a chair beneath the window, well away from the waiting customers.

"That's you," the old man whispered and pointed at the buffalo head. "You're useless. You allow people to hang their hats on you. They take away your land and it was your idea."

Maurice was stung. "It's necessary to build the dike," he said. "Where would we be without one? This town could never survive another flood like the last one. And I for one don't wish to go through that again." Like a knife, he comes through the bush sideways, his mother had said. He remembered this uncle only dimly as being a kind of vagabond. He would appear suddenly as in a dream at their door with a rabbit or a string of fish. Stay well away from that one, she'd warned him. He's more Indian than French.

"And you think a hill of dirt will stop the river?"

"But of course. It will be higher than the river will ever come."

"Then I've wasted my time. You're a foolish man. You will never have what is yours."

"You can't change history," Maurice said in an attempt to lighten the atmosphere. Now go. Go and leave me be.

As though reading his thoughts, the old man got up from the chair. "You know nothing of history," he said. "Did you know that your grandfather was a river man?"

Because his parents had died when he was a child, Maurice knew little about his relatives. He knew that his mother's people had come long before the settlers to the area that was now Grande Pointe. That they had been both hunters and farmers along the river, squatting on a large piece of land north of Agassiz about thirty miles. La Grande Pointe de la Saline, it was called for a time and then shortened to Grande Pointe when a town formed. His father's people had come from Quebec.

"Is that so?"

"It was during the time of the blue herons. Some say he rode those giant birds to the lake and back."

Maurice hid his smile. "You don't say? Rode the birds, eh?"

"And your great grandmother, she came from Buffalo Lake with ten children and a sick man. When he died, she kept herself and three families alive that winter with her snares."

Maurice swatted at an imaginary fly. "Ancient history," he said. "That has nothing whatsoever to do with me."

The men on the bench looked up from their newspapers as Desmarais walked over to the door. "We'll talk later," he said. "I'll wait for you at your house."

Oh God. No. "Wait," Maurice said. He could just see Mika's expression. He'd never told her about his mother. He'd let her think that both his parents were French. He put his hand on the man's arm. "I could get you a room here at the hotel," he said. "If you want to stay."

The old man stared at him for several moments. "You are saying I'm not welcome in your house?"

"Oh, it's not that. It's the little woman, she's busy with the children."

"You're like a raven caught in a thorn bush," Desmarais said. "I don't expect that anything will ever come from you. Much flapping of wings and that is all." He turned and left the barber shop as quietly as he'd come.

Maurice felt stricken, cut adrift. He wanted to follow the man, to explain. But his responsibilities kept him there. A newspaper crackled. Franklin cleared his throat impatiently. Maurice apologized for the delay. He picked up the clippers and went back to work.

The screen door was flung open with a bang.

"Hey Franklin, you'll never guess what we've found this time," a workman said. "Come and see."

Maurice followed along as the men ran down Main Street towards Agassiz Bridge and the ring dike. A group of them gathered on top of the unfinished dike in a circle, looking down at the ground. They were strange silhouettes against the red sky, motionless like granite headstones on a mound of black earth. Maurice didn't scramble and hurry with them. He felt that he knew what it was that they'd found. There had been many strange things, artifacts, pieces of pottery, arrowheads. He stepped into the circle of men. On the ground before them, partially buried, was the remains of a human.

"I called the RCMP," the workman said.

Maurice bent and examined the skull. It was porous and tinged brown from the earth. He felt sick. It could be the remains of one of his mother's people. One or his own people. "This is old," he said. "I guess these things happen when you're working that close to the cemetery. There are many lost markers, old grave sites that we don't know about." He stood up and wiped his hands on his pants. "But it's a good thing you called the police. Once they come, we can get on and bury it." He wished he knew something, anything, of his mother's people. He felt his loss in his fingertips; something important had slipped away from him like water through fingers, and he would never get it back.

Later that night, Maurice stood on the fire escape of the Scratching Chicken Hotel and leaned with his elbows against the railing. He was a little too drunk to go home yet. From his station, he could look out across the roofs of the houses, the skeletal frames of fresh lumber of the new ones, the bright yellow boards piercing together the older houses and grain elevators beyond them and far beyond the grain elevators, trees that were just faint brush strokes against the purple sky.

A sudden clinking noise in the alleyway below jolted him. He grasped the metal railing tightly. "Who's there?"

Since the flood, he scared easily. He often dreamed of drowning. Laurence Anderson emerged from the dark alleyway carrying two cartons of empty Coca-Cola bottles. He looked one way and then the other, failed to see Maurice above him, and ran down the street.

Maurice chuckled. It was just Johanna's boy; the mongrel was stealing cigarette money again. The boy was about fourteen years, he guessed, and had that clumsy knock-kneed gait of the half-grown. Because he had in the past slept with Johanna, he looked for his own features in the boy's face. But Laurence could be the kid of any one of dozens, he told himself. Maurice seemed to come upon him often in such out of the way places as the nuisance grounds, along the river, in the cemetery; and he was always alone, poking and turning things over. It was this roaming that reminded Maurice of himself.

Below him a fan churned out the smokey voices of the men in the parlour. There wasn't one distinguishable voice, the sounds were all mixed together, churning. The hotel had a new sign, it was a blinking neon chicken that had given the hotel its name, "Scratching Chicken." The chicken hunted and pecked out the words, EAT HERE, EAT HERE, EAT HERE. The sign, along with all the voices below him, mixed together as one, was to him a sign of progress. The town was booming. And he was part of it. He was accepted by the merchants along Main Street and it didn't help him one damned bit when people like Desmarais appeared on the scene like a scruffy spring rabbit.

Your worship, he said to himself, his mood swinging abruptly, as a member of this here town council, I would like to say that I think the flood had its benefits. Yessiree. On behalf of the children, old ladies and dogs, I propose that we install traffic lights at the corner. Slow those city buggers down when they come whipping through on the highway. He unzipped his fly. He laughed aloud. Your worship, as a member of the council, and in the interests of the people, I wish to bring to your attention the fact that people are pissing from the fire escape at the back of the hotel. Plain damned shame. Something should be done about it. Give everyone an umbrella.

Below him, the fan ceased moving. Closing time. Time to go home to the old lady. She'd be asleep, curled like a fist under the blankets on her side of the bed. He swayed unsteadily as he made his way down the fire escape. Hang on, or you're a gonner, he told himself. When he got home, he'd peel himself free from his barber shirt, search for stray hairs in his neck and go to bed. And then, yessiree, by God, whether she was sleeping or not, he'd tell her about old man Desmarais and about his mother.

The following morning, with a vague memory of his dreams of strange-looking blue birds sweeping low on water, Maurice got up, pushed aside the curtains in the bedroom and looked down into the garden. The winds had dispersed the smoke and the sunlight was not red anymore. But the squealing and rumbling of machinery continued. As he drew on his pants, the smell of lovemaking rose from his crotch like the smell of a catfish left lying on the riverbank. He would leave early, get a key for one of the rooms at the hotel and bathe. If he didn't, his customers would know for sure what he'd been into last night. He knew Mika would be angry this morning. He wondered: to go straight down and apologize or let her think he didn't remember what had happened? Whatever he chose, it could come later. He chose to delay facing Mika. He would instead go into the basement and search for his boots. He'd been meaning to have new clickers put on them.

As Maurice searched the corners of the basement for his boots, he heard Mika's feet slapping against the floor above his head and instantly he felt justified for his behaviour. The sound of her feet was as angry and unyielding as she'd been. She didn't keep herself the way other women did either. No rouge or powder, not even to please him. In better moments he could admit that he actually preferred her unpolished face, but not this morning. He stood debating, get it over with. Go on up there. Or pretend it didn't happen. He'd let himself get out of hand, to be sure. But part of it had been the beer, the other had been the old man coming to town. He heard the sounds of his children coming from every corner of the house. Too late. He'd have to wait.

"Well, how should I know where it is, you look for it." Mika's voice was raised suddenly, shattering the peacefulness of the basement.

"I did look for it," Lureen answered.

"Must I come?" It was a threat.

Lureen's tone matched her mother's. "I said I looked and so I did. I'm not lying."

"Alright then, I'll come," Mika said and Maurice heard her feet slap angrily across the kitchen floor. "But I'm warning you, if I find that shoe of yours, I'll give you such a smack for not looking for it properly. You have to get down on your knees when you look. You searched high and low, eh? We'll see about that."

She's still angry, Maurice thought. If apologizing would make life easier for her, he would do it. He was not one to mind going out of his way for another. It would make life easier for the children as well.

"Okay, okay. I'll look again," Lureen said and the rooms were calm once again as though a gust of wind had passed through them and gone. Then there was a soft murmur like dry leaves; Truda's voice, a halting search for words.

"I don't know what could have happened to your crayons," Mika said. Her voice was softer when she spoke to Truda. "Who would take them, a mouse?"

Peter the baby began to squall for attention. The remainder of their conversation was lost. Mika hurried across the kitchen. The cupboard door was opened, then closed. Maurice imagined her sprinkling puffed-wheat kernels across the tray for the baby to eat.

"Peter, Peter, pumpkin eater, had a wife and couldn't keep her," Mika said in a sing-song voice. The uneven legs of the highchair knocked against the floor as Mika jiggled it in time to her rhyme. "How are you this morning?" she asked the baby. "Eh? How is your little pumpkin, empty?"

Sharp rapid steps came from the corner of the dining room into the kitchen. Particles of dust floated downwards from the ceiling onto Maurice's neck. He rummaged about behind the furnace, searching for his army boots.

"Didn't I tell you?" Mika said, her voice harsh once again. "Get down on your hands and knees and you'll find your shoe. You kids. Now sit and eat."

It is only with the babies that she seems capable of gentleness, Maurice thought with sadness.

There were sounds of steps on the stairway as Betty came down from the top floor. "There you are, finally," Mika said. "You're always the last one. Today of all days to be late. Just when I've got so much to do. It's the Wednesday Circle today and it's my turn to have them here and you're late. Eat, while I braid your hair."

"I'm not hungry."

Mika sighed and it was felt all the way down Maurice's spine. Mika sighed when she kneaded bread at the table, she sighed when it rained, she sighed when the sun shone. When he had come home last night, she'd sighed as she stood before the mirror in their bedroom, unwinding her dark hair. When he curled against her back beneath the blankets and searched for words to tell her, my mother was an Indian, she'd mistaken his intentions. She sighed and said, no. Leave me be. Not until you install the kitchen window. And the anger had come rushing, thick and violent. He'd wanted to smash into her breasts with his fists but instead, he'd taken her with force, without using precautions, with a grinding punishing force that he felt in his own muscles this morning. His heart beat rose. He shook a cigarette loose from his package, struck his match against the basement wall. Today, he'd buy the lumber for the goddamned window and he would give her the morning sun.

"Have some cereal, even if you aren't hungry. You're the oldest. You set the example," Mika said. "If you go off to school without eating, then they'll want to, too."

"I'm your example to the whole world," Betty said. Maurice heard spoons clanking against bowls, saw mouths opening and closing, chewing, swallowing. He heard Sharon's dry cough echo in the furnace pipes and Rudy, who leaned against the door at the top of the basement stairs, bumping his head against it, signalling his need to use the toilet. He saw his boots hanging from a nail behind the furnace. He heard chairs scrape against the floor as the children gathered up their books and got up to leave for school. He dusted the boots off and slung them over his shoulder. It was time to go up there. He climbed the stairs slowly, dreading the initial contact with Mika's accusing eyes. If she had cried, anything, he would have been able to know how to approach her. This cold silence was another thing. He met Rudy on the stairs and ruffled his blonde head playfully. "Don't let the spiders get you, fella," he said.

Mika stood at the kitchen cupboard with her back to him. She balanced the baby on one hip. She hadn't rolled her hair up and it hung uncombed on her shoulders. He wanted to reach out and touch it. He liked seeing it hanging loose instead of rolled into that tight sausage ring at the back of her head. The first time she'd lain beside him, her head cradled into his shoulder like a small child, he thought that he'd never touched anything so fine and so soft as her hair. He took his sweater down from the wall behind the door. She heard the noise and turned. He steadied himself against her bitter tongue.

There were pouches of colour beneath her hazel eyes, like two bruises, but her face was calm. "On Saturday," she said, "the children are going to begin German lessons." She jostled the baby lightly.

German lessons? What now? "Is that so?"

"Yes. So, you don't mind, then? My father said he would take them on if I wanted. But he thought I should ask you first."

"Suit yourself." He was relieved. They were going to pretend it hadn't happened. "But what's the reasoning? I can count on one hand the number of people who speak German in this town."

She licked her fingers and began making a curl stand up on the baby's head. He saw a certain cunning in her expression. "It's not that. It's part of their background. I think they should have it while my father is still able to do it."

And suddenly he was angry. She'd denied him the presence of his brothers in his own home. She was going to teach the children to speak German. "Fine. And what should we teach them of my background?"

Her tightly contained anger broke loose. Her eyes became pinpoints of hostility. "What would you teach them?" she asked, spitting the words at him overtop the baby's head. "How to drink?"

"Listen here, my grandfather was a river man."

"I thought you said he came from Quebec."

"On my mother's side, I mean."

"That must have been before I came," she said. She dismissed anything that had happened before she'd come to Canada as being unimportant, not affecting her in any way. She shifted the baby to the other hip and brushed hair from her face. "Anyway," she said, ending their conversation, "anyway, it was the wrong time. It was the wrong time for you to forget yourself. I could get pregnant."

He was momentarily stunned. She always surprised him like this. She was more concerned about being pregnant than by what he'd done. He thought about the possibility. Seven kids. That would be embarrassing. People were beginning to make crude jokes about Mika's yearly swelling and popping of babies. "I didn't know. I'm sorry," he said.

"That won't do any good," she said.

He'd offered his hand and been bitten. "Don't bother with my breakfast," he said. "I can always get a bite to eat at the hotel." He had always been able to use Mika's strong jealousy as an effective means of retaliation. Johanna cooked at the hotel.

He thought she was going to throw the baby at him. "So go and eat, I don't care."

But he saw the fear in her eyes. He was not a heartless man. "By the way," he said, as he buttoned up his sweater, "send one of the girls to the shop after school. I'm going to need a hand carrying the lumber home." This talk of land, this mooning over old bones. Desmarais was far away and should stay there. You live what you know, he told himself, and what you don't, well, you can't be held accountable for that. He could feel Mika's attitude towards him change. Her features softened. She set the baby into the highchair.

"What for?" she asked. "Lumber for what?"

He told her what she wanted to hear. "For the window. I've been meaning to get at it for some time now."

She looked up at the clock above the sink. "There's still time," she said. "Let me poach you an egg."

He smiled and reached for her. He put his face into her soft hair. "If it's a girl," he said, "we'll name her Tina, after your aunt."

She struggled free. "Heaven forbid," she said. "If it's a a baby, I'll jump off the roof." But she wasn't angry anymore. She drew in her bottom lip, sucked at it, as though she'd only just remembered. "Did you telephone your brothers yet?"

"No, but I will today."

"What will you tell them?" she asked.

"I'll tell them there's a fly in the ointment."

She looked at him, puzzled. "I'll think of something," he said.

He watched as she prepared his food. She was strong and efficient and moved incredibly fast as she worked, and still she appeared to be small and often had the appearance of being lost, defenseless. It had taken him only one month to realize that she was as defenseless as a badger. His brothers had their wives and he had his and that was all any of them really had. He was joined together with her in the present. She was what he could put his hands on and touch. But he knew, for some reason, it would never be enough.

Truda

"IT'S TIME to do something about all your drawings,"
Mika said to Truda. She knelt on the floor searching the
bottom of the bedroom closet for plastic rain coats and hats.
"Cloudy, possible showers this morning, some sunny patches
in the southern regions, above normal temperatures," the
announcer said. The radio in Mika's bedroom was turned
up loud. Mika backed from the closet with a roll of Truda's
drawings in her hand.

"Look at this mess, will you? You can't keep these drawings
forever. The wax in the crayons will attract mice."

Mice had moved into the house during the flood, taking
over the top floor, eating all of Mika's plants down to the earth
in the pots and burrowing inside to get at the roots. Mice had
chewed holes in their curtains, pulled strips of wallpaper loose
from around the baseboards, gnawed at the plaster beneath,

leaving behind hollows lined with delicate grooves like veins in a leaf. The mice had also left behind a furry smell, a grey mouldy odour that Mika scrubbed free with Lysol. Mika had worked diligently, had reclaimed the house from the flood waters, and the mice had been banished, nothing of them remained except for the imagined fine whiskers twitching in the corners, the soft scurrying in the dust beneath the bed at night.

"I don't think mice like wax," Truda said.

"Mice or no mice, you can't keep all these drawings. It's getting out of hand. That's all you do, day and night, and it's not good for your eyes."

Truda was the only Lafreniere to wear glasses. Her mother couldn't understand it. Lack of carrots, her father said. Not only do carrots give you good eyesight, they also give you hair on your chest. Look at me, Maurice said, living proof. Swallow a fruit pit and a tree will grow inside, bee stings are really smooches for sweet children. Truda doubted it. She knew the reason for her poor eyesight. At one time, she'd cried too much.

Mika unrolled the drawings and spread them across the floor. "Where did you ever get all the paper?" she asked. She was practical, wondered more about the gathering of paper rather than why or what was in the drawings.

Truda couldn't decide whether or not to answer. She ran her tongue across her top teeth to keep the words inside. It was still easier for her to remain silent than it was to speak. When she sat at the washstand on her stool facing the window drawing pictures, she could go the whole day without speaking to anyone.

"From the bakeshop. The girl gave it to me."

"You crossed the highway alone?"

Caught. Truda felt sweat on her palms. Words were traps. "Betty came with me."

"That's neither here nor there. You can't keep every single drawing. Pick out the best ones and throw the rest out."

"I can't."

"There's no such word as can't."

Then why did you just use it yourself, Truda wondered.

"I didn't say to get rid of all of them. Just some, okay? Where would I be if everyone collected junk? Snowed under." Mika began shuffling through the drawings as though looking for some redeemable quality that might justify keeping them. She looked for genius and saw crude shapes of houses, barns, farm machinery, gardens, chickens. She picked out a drawing, pointed to the figure of a young girl. "Is this you?" she asked. "Have you drawn yourself into the pictures? Is that why you want to keep them?"

Of course it's not me. How could she be so ridiculous? The girl had black curly hair, she didn't wear glasses. "No, that's not me."

The pictures were drawings of the farm where she'd stayed during the flood. The girl was the one who'd been in the photograph on the piano with her eyes closed, a circle of flowers in her hair. Truda gathered the drawings together quickly. But Mika's attention had already begun to wander. "Where did I put those rain coats?" she asked herself. She got up from the floor and stepped over Truda. "Well, do what you want. But if you spent as much energy running and playing as you do on these drawings, then you wouldn't be so fat."

Truda didn't mind. She knew her mother's comment was punishment for not being agreeable, but she was able to keep the drawings. She listened as Mika went downstairs. She heard Lureen talking in the kitchen below. That was the way she liked the house to be. She preferred to be alone and still have people moving about, talking to each other. If she stayed in her room drawing and suddenly it grew silent beneath her, she went looking until she found them. She rolled up the drawings. She would need to find a safe place for them some-where against any tampering that could later be blamed on a mouse, in the same way silence could be blamed on a cat.

"Oh good, you're here, finally," Mika said as Truda entered the kitchen. "Have some cereal."

Truda ate the cold breakfast cereal without tasting the blue-tinged powdered milk or the dry papery flavour of the puffed wheat kernels. She closed out the voices of her brothers and sisters and planned her next drawing. Everything about the farm had been backwards. When you came in the door there were latches on the wall in the porch. Latches that held brooms and mops firmly snapped into place. In one corner had been the cream separator with a checkered cloth draped over the bowl and in the other corner, a blue metal pie plate on the floor and cats feeding around it, wild frightened cats that zig-zagged out of her path when she entered the porch.

"I've got a job for you to do today," Mika said to Truda.

"I was going to ask if Truda could come with me after school when I go for the eggs," Betty said.

"Afraid to go alone?" Lureen's voice was strident. "What a suck."

"Well, sorry, but Truda can't go with you. I need her to pull weeds in the garden."

"How come?" Lureen asked. "Why do I have to stay in after school and wash sealers in the basement while Truda gets to do the garden? It's not fair. I always do the garden."

Their voices jabbed against Truda like a fork stabbing peas on a plate. There had been a window above the cats' feeding dish. And dried-up flies cradled in a spider's web. When you entered the farm house, instead of the kitchen there was a large dining room filled with dark furniture. Then to the left, sliding doors, a cramped parlour, a piano with a photograph of a young girl in a coffin. Stop: before that, the yard. She needed to remember the yard. She needed to reconstruct all parts of the farm because although she'd lived there almost six months, it was as though it had been a dream. She looked up at the refrigerator where she kept the bucket of crayons, out of reach of the little ones who would colour the walls or eat the crayons, Mika said. They were gone.

"My crayons," Truda said. Had Mika discovered the way to stop the drawings?

"Look here," Mika said to Lureen. "If you'd done a better job weeding the garden last time, you'd be doing it now. Besides, it won't hurt Truda to get some fresh air."

"My crayons are missing."

"If Truda can come with me to get the eggs, I'll help her do the garden," Betty said.

"Well, I'm not sitting in this dumb house all day washing jars. What about my fresh air, eh? I could die down there. Why is it only Truda who needs fresh air?"

"You'll do as I tell you."

A spoon clattered to the floor. "And where are you off to?" Mika asked Truda. Truda was halfway across the kitchen.

"To look for my crayons. They're gone. Someone took them."

"Who would take them, a mouse?" Mika asked. "You don't need your crayons this very minute. Come and sit down. Don't slow things down; I've got so much to do." She turned to Betty. "Alright, I don't care. Truda can go with you just as long as everything gets done."

My crayons, my crayons, Truda thought. She's taken them. Mika reached for the Bible resting on top of the radio. She set the Bible down on the table with a thump and opened it to the place where a bay leaf had been stuck between the pages as a marker.

Thou shalt not steal, Truda thought. The delicate scent of the bay leaf was released as Mika began to read.

After school Truda and Betty walked along the highway to the small yellow cottage where Betty would pick up three dozen eggs. "I know it was her," Truda said. "I know she took my crayons." They had walked two blocks and then the houses dwindled and gave way to open fields. Their running shoes and legs were covered in a yellow dust from the fresh gravel on the shoulder of the road. Truda walked with her head down. She'd once seen a boy at school catch the sun in a glass and beneath the glass, paper smouldered and burned. The same thing would happen to her eyes if she looked at the sun. She disliked the clicking sounds that the grasshoppers made in the ditch along the highway. At the farm, she'd had an insect jump down the front of her dress. They'd laughed, teased her, took her dress off in the middle of the field. It wasn't pleasant laughter, but nevertheless it had been laughter which was scarce on the farm where everyone had their job to do and did it as though tomorrow wouldn't come if they didn't. In the small cramped parlour, the photograph of the little girl, and also on top of the piano, the mantle clock, striking the hour as she entered the house. Each time it bonged, the sound froze her mind. The sound of it was an old yellowing wooden sound and a lemon polish, warm milk and silverware cleaner sound. Beyond the kitchen, stairs to the attic had black rubber treads with grooves in them that made her think, black licorice; but they weren't that, they tasted bitter when she put her tongue on them.

> I'm coming up one step—dropping buns
> I'm coming up two steps—dropping buns
> I'm coming up three steps—dropping buns
> I'm coming up fourteen steps—dropping buns
> And there I met a horse who was—dropping buns.

The attic: along one wall, a chest with an embroidered cloth on top of it. A fold-down cot with a crochet spread beside a mangle iron.

"She doesn't want me to draw and so she took away my crayons," Truda said.

Betty squeezed Truda's hand. "She only put them away for the summer. Wait and see."

"I want to go home." And look for them.

"Well you can't. And there's a lot to see outside of your room if you'd only look." Betty nudged Truda's chin upwards. "Look, what do you see?"

She saw nothing. Fields, the sky. At the farm, a strange humming sound had risen up out of the fields and the people on the fields were like specks of dust moving across the horizon into the midst of the humming. And then she saw something else, like water, running overtop the highway. It sparkled and jumped beneath the sun. It was glassy blue and spilled off the highway into the fields. "A lake," she said. "I see a lake."

Betty laughed. "That's what I thought too when I first saw it. But it isn't a lake. I've been out there and you know, it gets further away, you can never reach it."

"I see waves," Truda said. She was excited. They thought she was still blind. They forgot, she could see now, even the leaves on the trees. And she could see the lake. It wasn't the yellowish brown of the river either, creeping up step by step until they'd had to climb into a boat and paddle away from town. The lake was like Betty's eyes, it was glassy blue.

"What you see are heat waves rising off the highway. I don't know how it happens. It just does." They crossed the highway and approached the cottage where Betty would get the eggs.

"But it looks real, like a lake."

Betty led Truda down into the shallow ditch beside the highway. A car shot past and Truda watched as the car met the lake on the highway, cut through and vanished. "Come," Betty said. "We'll sit for a while and rest our legs." She set the cartons down and flopped back into the grass. Truda lay down beside

her. She heard the humming sound coming up from the fields.
She heard the cry of the Franklin gulls and shaded her eyes to
find them.

She had sat on the cot in the attic room at the farm and
listened to the birds circling above the fields. The farm woman
was awkward, thought Truda couldn't dress herself and complained as she forced Truda's arms into the armholes of a
cotton blouse she'd ironed on the mangle. The cotton squeaked
as the buttons were pushed through holes which were too small.
The blouse was the colour of goldenrod. It belonged to the
dead girl on the piano. Draw: birds, grey with some blue shining in the grey wings. Their beaks made funny *kapoka* sounds
on the gravel. They muttered and complained and once she
thought she'd heard her name mentioned. She stood still, heart
pumping blood wildly, fearful that they would smell her and
fly away. The people were all on the fields. They were the
specks in the dust coming to the house when they had breakdowns or for the prepared food. It made it easier to keep her
vow not to speak when there was no one to talk to, except for
the birds. She scooped chicken feed from the sack and scattered
it around the yard. She moved among the birds slowly, speaking
the sad soft cooing call of the male, and they rose up quickly,
their wings fanning the air. She followed them, wheeling over
the blue spruce, the willows at the far end of the pond, across
the fields spread out below, golden patches on a huge quilt of
green and blue, to Agassiz. To her home and her family.

Truda raised her arm and followed a single bird's flight
with a finger, guided it down towards the lake but at the last
moment, it veered away. She thought she could hear waves
and the sound of it reminded her of the flood. She felt as though
she carried her own Franklin gull sound inside her chest, over-
whelming her with its terrible lonely cry. It was how she'd felt
when she'd been at the farm, awake in the attic, waiting and
waiting for the flood to be finished.

"Guess what, Truda? You have a new baby brother. I've named him Peter. Isn't that wonderful?" Static on the telephone wire, it was the sparrows bouncing on the wire outside the window, making Mika's words break into fragments...guess... baby...wonder....

I said. I said. I said. I said. The sparrows one after another fluttered from the wire. It shivered, a silver arc, then it straightened and dissolved into the sky. Silence.

"I said, don't leave me here. When are you coming to get me?"

"Have you got nothing to say? Cat's got your tongue?"

"Don't worry, it's a little thing," the farm woman said. "Once you come she'll find her tongue again. We didn't want to worry you. It's a little thing and you have your hands full with the new baby."

After that, the rain began falling, making everything blurred around the edges and so she missed seeing her mother's face at the car window. She had stood crying in the house, looking out across the yard at the road through a rain-spattered window and it was the flood. That's what made everything so wet. That and her crying. The rain came and the road past the house dissolved and oozed black dirt into deep waterfilled gulleys on each side. A man pushed the car down the road away from the farm. They couldn't stop and come for her because of the new baby, the slippery road, the rain, the flood, her crying. Even though it was her seventh birthday, and they'd promised to come, they didn't stop. And so she didn't get to see her mother's white moonshaped face at the car window. Look, look, she's waving, someone said. But Truda doubted it. See, there's your mother, girl. Stop crying for once. Don't you know, water attracts water? But she couldn't stop crying and so her two weeks' stay turned into three months and then another three months. Crying made everything worse. She'd ruined her eyes.

Ooowee, oowee, the gull inside her chest cried. *Ooowee.*

"Did you know that this land was once all under water?" Betty asked. "Once upon a time it was a large lake."

Happy Birthday to you, crying made everything worse. But she'd discovered that crayons and paper made it better. Drawing was a bird moving against a clean sky the way you wanted it to.

"Hey, you sleeping?"

"Next time, take me with you," Truda said. "I don't want to go to the farm. I'll run away if they make me stay there. Next time—"

Betty laughed and slid her arm beneath Truda's neck, pulling her head onto her shoulder. "What's this next time business? We probably won't have another flood. And even if we do, we have the dikes now. So forget about the flood once and for all and listen. Thousands of years ago, this was all lake. Lake Agassiz." Betty sat up and pointed across the fields. "A hundred miles away is the nearest shoreline. In the Pembina Hills. Miss Janzen showed us on a map at school."

"Will it ever come back?" Like the flood, a trickle first across the basement floor and later, a rushing waterfall and sealers bobbing about in the muddy water.

Betty gathered the egg cartons up and got to her feet. "No, it won't come back. Not in a million years. We've got nothing to worry about." She pulled Truda's ear. They crossed planks that led across the ditch to the yellow cottage. They stopped outside the gate.

"Like it out here?" Betty asked.

"Yes." The sun didn't hurt her eyes the way she thought it would.

"Good. Wait until the flax is blooming. It looks just like a lake too."

"There is a lake out there. I can hear waves."

"It's all in your head, believe me," Betty said. "Now wait right here. I won't be long."

Truda waited. She leaned into the fence and looked at the lake. It jumped forward and channels of water tipped down the highway towards her. It was all in her head but she could smell fish and see shells and sand. The gulls flew low, crossing and crisscrossing each other's flight paths. She could see their black feet tucked up against white-grey bottoms. She looked down and saw milky water receding before her feet, leaving wet crescent marks on the ends of her navy sneakers. Beige sand, dappled with curious flat grey pebbles, rounded perfectly smooth, was left in the water's wake. She stooped, picked several pebbles and dropped them into her pocket before the white frothy water rushed back up, cold, overtop her shoes and then up around her ankles. She lifted her eyes to the lake. The gulls cried with joy and bounced their solid bodies against the lake. It was like nothing she had ever drawn. She didn't need crayons when she had all this in her head. Mika could never take away her head. Her own gull rose. She felt the cold water around her calves, at her knees and then it swirled about her thighs. She took a deep breath and dove under. She didn't need to draw the farm. The farm was gone and her imagination was a tree growing inside and green leaves unfolding one by one.

The Wednesday Circle

BETTY crosses the double planks that span the ditch in front of Joys' yard. Most people have only one plank. But Mrs. Joy needs two. Mrs. Joy is a possible candidate for the circus. Like sleeping with an elephant, Betty's father says often. But Mr. and Mrs. Joy, the egg people, don't sleep together. Betty knows this even though she's never gone further than inside their stale smelling kitchen.

The highway is a smeltering strip of gunmetal grey at her back. It leads to another town like the one she lives in. If you kept on going south, you would get to a place called Pembina in the States and a small dark tavern where a woman will serve under-age kids beer. Laurence, Betty's friend, knows about this. But if you turn from the highway and go west, there are dozens of villages and then the Pembina Hills which Betty has seen on one occasion, a school trip to the man-made lake at Morden. Home of the rich and the godly, Betty's father calls these villages. Wish the godly would stay home. Can't get a seat in the parlour on Friday nights.

Beyond her lies a field in summer fallow and a dirt road rising to a slight incline and then falling as it meets the highway. Before her is the Joys' crumbling yellow cottage, flanked on all sides by greying bales of straw which have swollen and broken free from their bindings and are scattered about the yard. Behind the cottage is the machine shed. Behind the machine shed and bumping up against the prairie is the chicken coop.

Because Mika, Betty's mother, sends her for the eggs instead of having them delivered by Mr. Joy, she gets them cheaper.

Betty balances the egg cartons beneath her chin and pushes open the gate. It shrieks on its rusty hinges. The noise doesn't affect her as it usually does. Usually, the noise is like a door opening into a dark room and she is filled with dread. Today, she is prepared for it. Today is the day for the Wednesday Circle. The church ladies are meeting at her home. Even now, they're there in the dining room, sitting in a circle with their Bibles in their laps. It's like women and children in the centre. And arrows flying. Wagons are going up in flames and smoke. The goodness and matronly wisdom of the Wednesday Circle is a newly discovered thing. She belongs with them now. They can reach out to protect her even here, by just being what they are. And although she wants nothing to happen today, she is prepared for the worst.

"Come on in," Mrs. Joy calls from the kitchen.

Betty sets the egg cartons down on the steps and enters the house. Mrs. Joy's kitchen resembles a Woolworth store. There are porcelain dogs and cats in every corner on knick knack shelves. Once upon a time, she used to love looking at those figurines but now she thinks they're ugly.

The woman sits in her specially made chair which is two chairs wired together. Her legs are stretched out in front resting up on another chair. Out of habit, Betty's heart constricts because she knows the signs. Mrs. Joy is not up to walking back to the chicken coop with her. And that's how it all began.

"Lo, I am with you always even unto the end of the world," her mind recites.

These verses rise unbidden. She has memorized one hundred of them and won a trip to a summer Bible camp at Lake Winnipeg. She has for the first time seen the ocean on the prairie and tried to walk on water. The waves have lifted and pulled her out where her feet couldn't touch the sandy bottom and she has been swept beneath that mighty sea and heard the roaring of the waves in her head and felt the sting of fish water in her nostrils. Like a bubble of froth she is swept beneath the water, back and forth by the motion of the waves. She is drowning. What happens is just as she's heard. Her whole life flashes by. Her head becomes a movie screen playing back every lie and swearing, malicious and unkind deeds, thoughts, words. There is not one thing that makes her look justified for having done or said them. And then her foot touches a rock and she pushes herself forward in desperation, hoping it's the right direction.

Miraculously, it is. She bounces forward from the depths to where she can tip-toe to safety, keeping her nose above the waves. She runs panting with fear to her cabin. She pulls the blankets over her. She tells no one. But that evening in the chapel during devotions, the rustling wind in the poplars against the screen causes her to think of God. When they all sing, "Love Lifted Me," the sunset parts the clouds above the water so there is a crack of gold where angels hover, watching. So she goes forward to the altar with several others and has her name written in the Book of Life. They tell her the angels are clapping and she thinks she can hear them there at that crack of gold which is the door to heaven. She confesses every sin she's been shown in the water except for one. For some reason, it wasn't there in the movie. And they are such gentle, smiling nice people who have never done what she's done. So she can't bring herself to tell them that Mr. Joy puts his hands in her pants.

"Rainin' today, ain't it child?" Mrs. Joy asks.

"No, not yet," Betty says. "It's very muggy."

"Don't I know it," she says.

"Are your legs sore?" Betty asks.

"Oh Lord, yes, how they ache," Mrs. Joy says and rolls her eyes back into her head. Her jersey dress is a tent stretched across her knees. She cradles a cookie tin in her lap.

"That's too bad," Betty says.

A chuckle comes from deep inside her mammoth chest. "You sound just like your mother," she says. "And you're looking more and more like her each time I see you. You're just like an opal, always changing."

God's precious jewels, Mrs. Joy calls them when she visits Mika. She lines them up verbally, Betty and her sisters and brothers, comparing chins, noses. This one here, she says about Betty, she's an opal. You oughta keep a watch over that one. Always changing. But it just goes to show, His mysteries does He perform. Not one of them the same.

"Thank you," Betty says, but she hates being told she looks like her mother. Mika has hazel eyes and brown hair. She is blonde and blue-eyed like her Aunt Elizabeth.

"Well, you know where the egg pail is," Mrs. Joy says, dismissing her with a flutter of her pudgy hand.

"Aren't you coming?" Betty asks.

"Not today, girl. It aches me so to walk. You collect the eggs and then you jest find Mr. Joy and you pay him. He gets it in the end anyhow."

Betty looks around the kitchen. His jacket is missing from its hook on the wall. She goes over to the corner by the window and feigns interest in the porcelain figures. She picks one up, sets it down. His truck is not in the yard.

"Where is he?"

"Went to town for something," Mrs. Joy says. "But I thought he'd be back by now. Doesn't matter though, jest leave the money in the back porch."

The egg pail thumps against her leg as she crosses the yard to the chicken coop. She walks towards the cluttered wire enclosure, past the machine shed. The doors are open wide. The hens scratch and dip their heads in her direction as she approaches. Hope rises like an erratic kite as she passes the shed and there are no sounds coming from it. She stamps her feet and the hens scatter before her, then circle around and approach her from behind, silently. She quickly gathers three dozen of the warm, straw-flecked eggs, and then steps free of the stifling smelly coop out into the fresh moist air. She is almost home-free. She won't have to face anything today. It has begun to rain. Large spatters spot her white blouse, feel cool on her back. She sets the pail down on the ground beside the egg cartons and begins to transfer the eggs.

"Here, you don't have to do that outside." His sudden voice, as she fills the egg cartons, brings blood to her face, threatens to pitch her forward over the pail.

He strides across the yard from the shed. "Haven't got enough sense to come in out of the rain," he says. "Don't you know you'll melt? Be nothing left of you but a puddle."

He carries the pail, she carries the cartons. He has told her: Mrs. Joy is fat and lazy, you are my sunshine, my only sunshine. I would like six little ones running around my place too, but Mrs. Joy is fat and lazy. His thin hand has gone from patting her on the head with affection, to playfully slapping her on the behind, graduated then to tickling her armpits and ribs and twice now, his hands have been inside her underpants.

"Be not afraid," a verse leaps into her head. "For I am with you." She will put her plan into action. The Wednesday Circle women are strong and mighty. She knows them all, they're her mother's friends. She'll just go to them and say, Mr. Joy feels me up, and that will be the end of it.

She walks behind him, her heart pounding. He has an oil rag hanging from his back pocket and his boots are caked with clay, adding inches to his height.

"I'm waiting for my parts," he says over his shoulder. "Can't do anything until I get that truck fixed." Sometimes he talks to her as though she were an adult. Sometimes as though she were ten again and just coming for the eggs for the first time. How old are you, he'd asked the last time and was surprised when she said, fourteen. My sunshine has grown up.

They enter the machine shed and he slides the doors closed behind them, first one and then the other, leaving a sliver of daylight beaming through where the doors join. A single light bulb dangles from a wire, shedding a circle of weak yellow light above the truck, not enough to clear the darkness from the corners.

"Okay-dokey," he says and puts the pail of eggs on the workbench. "You can work here. I've got things to do." He goes over to the truck, disappears beneath its raised hood.

Then he's back at the workbench, searching through his tool box. "Seen you with your boyfriend the other day," he says. "That Anderson boy."

"He's not my boyfriend," she says.

"I saw you," he says. His usual bantering tone is missing. "The two of you were in the coulee." Then his breath is warm on the side of her face as he reaches across her. His arm knocks against her breast, sending pain shooting through her chest.

I need a bra, she has told Mika. Whatever for? Wear an undershirt if you think you really need to.

"Do you think it's a good idea to hang around in the coulee with your boyfriend?"

"He's not my boyfriend," she says. "I told you."

He sees her flushed cheeks, senses her discomfort. "Aha," he says. "So he is. You can't fool me."

She moves away from him. Begins to stack the cartons up against her chest, protection against his nudgings. Why is it that everyone but her own mother notices that she has breasts now?

"Don't rush off," he says. "Wait until the rain passes." The sound of it on the tin roof is like small pebbles being dropped one by one.

He takes the cartons from her and sets them back on the workbench. He smiles and she can see that perfect decayed circle between his front teeth. His hair is completely grey even though he's not as old as her father. He starts to walk past her, back towards the truck and then suddenly he grasps her about the waist and begins to tickle her ribs. She is slammed up against him and gasping for breath. His whiskers prickle against her neck. She tastes the bitterness of his flannel shirt.

She pushes away. "Stop."

He holds her tighter. "You're so pretty," he says. "No wonder the boys are chasing you. When I'm working in here, know what I'm thinking all the time?"

"Let me go." She continues to push against his bony arms.

"I'm thinking about all the things I could do to you."

Against her will, she has been curious to know. She feels desire rising when he speaks of what he would like to do. He has drawn vivid word-pictures that she likes to reconstruct until her face burns. Only it isn't Mr. Joy in the pictures, it's Laurence. It's what made her pull aside her underpants so he could fumble inside her moist crevice with his grease-stained fingers.

"Show me your tits," he whispers into her neck. "I'll give you a dollar if you do."

She knows the only way out of this is to tell. When the whole thing is laid out before the Wednesday Circle, she will become whiter than snow. "No," she says.

"What do you mean, no," he says, jabbing her in the ribs once again.

"I'm going to tell," she says. "You can't make me do anything anymore because I'm going to tell on you." She feels as though a rock has been taken from her stomach. He is ugly. He is like a salamander dropping from the sky after a rainstorm into a mincemeat pail. She doesn't know how she could ever have liked him.

"Make you?" he says. "Make you? Listen here, girlie, I've only done what you wanted me to do."

She knows this to be true and not true. She isn't certain how she has come to accept and even expect his fondling. It has happened over a course of four years, gradually, like growing.

She walks to the double doors where the light shines through. "Open them, please," she says.

"Open them yourself," he says. She can feel the presence of the Wednesday Circle. The promise of their womanly strength is like a lamp unto her feet. They will surround her and protect her. Freedom from his word-pictures will make her a new person.

"You say anything," he says. "You say one thing and I'll have some pretty stories to tell about you. You betcha."

"That woman," Mika is saying to the Wednesday Circle as Betty enters the dining room. "That woman. She has absolutely no knowledge of the scriptures. She takes everything out of context." Mika is standing at the buffet with a china tea cup in her hand. Betty steps into the circle of chairs and sits down in Mika's empty one. Mika stops talking, throws her a look of surprise and question. The other women greet her with smiles, nods.

"Did you get the eggs?" Mika asks.

Betty feels her mouth stretching, moving of its own accord into a silly smile. She knows the smile irritates Mika but she can't help it. At times like these, her face moves on its own. She can hear her own heartbeat in her ears, like the ocean, roaring.

"What now?" Mika asks, worried.

"What do you mean, she takes everything out of context?" Mrs. Brawn asks, ignoring Betty. It's her circle. She started it off, arranging for the church women to meet in each others' homes twice a month to read scripture and sew things which they send to a place in the city where they are distributed to the poor. The women are like the smell of coffee to Betty and at the same time, they are like the cool opaque squares of Mika's lemon slice which is arranged on bread and butter plates on the table. They are also like the sturdy varnished chairs they sit on. To be with them now is the same as when she was a child and thought that if you could always be near an adult when you were ill, you wouldn't die.

"My, my," Mika mimics someone to demonstrate to Mrs. Brawn what she means. She places her free hand against her chest in a dramatic gesture. "They are different, ain't they? God's precious jewels. Just goes to show, His mysteries does He perform."

Betty realizes with a sudden shock that her mother is imitating Mrs. Joy.

Mrs. Brawn takes in Mika's pose with a stern expression and immediately Mika looks guilty, drops her hand from her breast and begins to fill cups with coffee.

"I suppose that we really can't expect much from Mrs. Joy," Mika says with her back to them. Betty hears the slight mocking tone in her voice that passes them by.

Heads bent over needlework nod their understanding. The women's stitches form thumbs, forest-green fingers; except for the woman who sits beside Betty. With a hook she shapes intricate spidery patterns to lay across varnished surfaces, the backs of chairs. What the poor would want with those, I'll never know, Mika has said privately. But they include the doilies in their parcels anyway because they have an understanding. They whisper that this white-haired woman has known suffering.

She works swiftly. It seems to Betty as though the threads come from the ends of her fingers, white strings with a spot of red every few inches. It looks as though she's cut her finger and secretly bleeds the colour into the lacy scallops. The women all unravel and knit and check closely for evenness of tension.

Mika enters the circle of chairs then, carrying the tray of coffee, and begins to make her way around it. She continues to speak of Mrs. Joy.

"Are you looking forward to school?" the white-haired woman asks Betty. Her voice is almost a whisper, a knife peeling skin from a taut apple. Betty senses that it has been difficult for her to speak, feels privileged that she has.

"Yes, I miss school."

The woman blinks as she examines a knot in her yarn. She scrapes at it with her large square thumbnail which is flecked oddly with white fish-hook-shaped marks. "Your mother tells us you were at camp," she says. "What did you do there?"

Mika approaches them with the tray of coffee. "I just wish she hadn't picked me out, that's all," Mika says. "She insists on coming over here in the morning and it's impossible to work with her here. And Mr. Joy is just as bad. I send Betty for the eggs now because he used to keep me at the door talking."

Mr. Joy is just as bad. Mr. Joy makes me ashamed of myself and I let him do it. The woman shakes loose the doily; it unfolds into the shape of a star as she holds it up.

"You like it?" the white-haired woman asks Betty.

"It's pretty."

"Maybe I give it to you."

"Ah, Mika," a woman across the circle says, "she just knows where she can find the best baking in town."

Then they all laugh; even the quiet woman beside Betty has a dry chuckle over the comment, only Mrs. Brawn doesn't smile. She stirs her coffee with more force than necessary and sets the spoon alongside it with a clang.

"Obesity is no laughing matter," she says. "Mrs. Joy is a glutton and that's to be pitied. We don't laugh at sin, the wages of sin is death."

"But the gift of God is eternal life through Jesus Christ our Lord," the woman says so softly, the words are nail filings dropping into her lap. If Betty hadn't seen her lips moving, she wouldn't have heard it. "God forgives," the woman says then, louder. She is an odd combination of young and old. Her voice and breasts are young but her hair is white.

Mika stands before them with the tray of coffee. "Not always," Mika says. "There's the unpardonable sin, don't forget about that." She seems pleased to have remembered this.

"Which is?" the woman asks.

"Well, suicide," Mika says. "It has to be, because when you think of it, it's something you can't repent of once the deed is done." Mika smiles around the circle as if to say to them, see, I'm being patient with this woman who has known suffering.

"Perhaps there is no need to repent," the woman says.

"Pardon?"

"In Russia," the woman begins and then stops to set her thread down into her lap. She folds her hands one on top of the other and closes her eyes. The others, sensing a story, fall silent.

"During the revolution in Russia, there was once a young girl who was caught by nine soldiers and was their prisoner for two weeks. She was only thirteen. These men had their way with her many times, each one taking their turn, every single night. In the end, she shot herself. What about her?"

"I've never heard of such a case," Mika says. She sounds as though she resents hearing of it now.

"There are always such cases," the woman says. "If God knows the falling of a single sparrow, He is also merciful. He knows we're only human."

Mrs. Brawn sets her knitting down on the floor in front of her chair, leans forward slightly. "Oh, He knows," she says. "But He never gives us more than we can bear. When temptation arises, He gives us the strength to resist." She closes her statement with her hands, like a conductor pinching closed the last sound.

Betty watches as the white-haired woman twists and untwists her yarn into a tight ring around her finger. "I don't believe for one moment," she says finally, "that God would condemn such a person to hell. Jesus walked the earth and so He knows."

"No, no," Mika says from the buffet. "He doesn't condemn us, don't you see? That's where you're wrong. We condemn ourselves. We make that choice."

"And what choice did that young girl have?" the woman asks. "It was her means of escape. God provided the gun."

Mika holds the tray of lemon squares up before her as though she were offering them to the sun. She looks stricken. Deep lines cut a sharp V above her nose. "You don't mean that," she says. "Suicide is unpardonable. I'm sure of it. Knowing that keeps me going. Otherwise, I would have done it myself long ago."

There is shocked silence and a rapid exchange of glances around the circle, at Betty, to see if she's heard.

"You shouldn't say such things," Mrs. Brawn says quietly. "For shame. You have no reason to say that."

The white-haired woman speaks with a gaunt smile. "Occasionally," she says, "in this room, someone dares to speak the truth."

"What do you mean?" asks Mrs. Brawn.

"Look at us," the woman says. "We're like filthy rags to Him in our self-righteousness. We obey because we fear punishment, not because we love."

Betty sees the grease spot on her blouse where his arm has brushed against her breast. Her whole body is covered in handprints. The stone is back in her stomach. She feels betrayed. For a moment the women are lost inside their own thoughts and they don't notice as she rises from her chair and sidles over to the door. Then, as if on some signal, their conversation resumes its usual level, each one waiting impatiently for the other to be finished so they can speak their words. Their laughter and goodwill have a feeling of urgency, of desperation. Betty stands at the door; a backward glance and she sees the white-haired woman bending over her work once again, eyes blinking rapidly, her fingers moving swiftly and the doily, its flecked pattern spreading like a web across her lap.

Stones

MOTHER made a new apron the day after she and Father quarrelled and he slammed the door and went walking. She didn't come away from the kitchen window for a long time, and I tip-toed around the house feeling nervous because she hadn't noticed that it was past my bedtime.

She was wearing the apron when she met the doctor's wife, Mrs. Hallman, out by the clothes line, only you couldn't see it for the pouch of clothespegs tied around her thick waist. Mrs. Hallman stood tall and slim, her red toenails sticking out the end of her white sandals and she smelled like the sweet william that grew in a patch beside the back porch. I hung around like a sticky fly in August and listened while they talked. Mother played with the pegs in the pouch and made little squares in the dirt with her foot while Mrs. Hallman said how pleased she was to be living in the country instead

of the city, so much nicer for the children, didn't she think?
Then she asked which one I was and Mother told her, Lureen
the second of five and one was coming.

Mrs. Hallman said, "Oh how nice," her Jane Russell lips
forming a raspberry circle and I wished suddenly that Mother
would take off the pouch so the ric rac on the apron would
show. Mrs. Hallman patted her flat stomach and told Mother
that it sure was good to be slim again and that was *it* for her.
Then she laughed and her voice went high and tinkly like a
wind chime. Mother laughed too, and her laughter was like
rubbing two stones together.

At supper Mother said to Father that the kids were terrible.
And how could she invite Mrs. Hallman in? He hadn't built
the cage he'd promised now for a month and Rudy let Jeepers
loose again in the kitchen and Sharon wouldn't come down
from the kitchen table. She'd offered Mrs. Hallman some
tomatoes, but they're allergic to tomatoes, and it was too bad,
but she couldn't play bridge with Mrs. Hallman because she
had better things to do with her time.

When Mrs. Hallman came for coffee, Mother would send
me to the cellar for a jar of jelly and spread a clean tablecloth.
Then she would sit drawing circles with her finger, smiling
and nodding while Mrs. Hallman rattled her charm bracelet
and talked about Toronto and Minneapolis and "my husband
the doctor." I would sit listening to her wind chime laughter,
unable to move when told to go out and play with the others.

When Mrs. Hallman left, Mother would bang pots and
pans on the stove or put on Father's fishing hat and chop weeds
in the garden, making chunks of earth fly up around her feet.

The oldest daughter, Emily, and I became friends. She
played store with real groceries and let me watch. She had
bubble gum and pop whenever she wanted and sometimes
gave me sips. She had her own bicycle and she wouldn't let me
ride it. I gave up my perch in the maple tree where I'd spent

he summer building a tree house and began moping about he kitchen complaining of having nothing to do. When I sked Mother why we didn't have one measly bike, she slamned the oven door hard and said stoves were more important han bicycles and if we ever got anything new around this house t would be a stove that works right.

Then Rudy tried fly casting at the telephone wires and aught a fish hook in his finger. Mother sent me to the Hall-nans' and the doctor said he'd come over and then stayed to ave a slice of fresh bread, his eyes never leaving the cupboard vhere Mother had piled her batches of bread and buns. And vhen he asked if it was really true, did she really make that lelicious bread, she smiled at him the way she smiles at Father vhen he pulls the little curl on the back of her neck and says he's keeping her girlish figure.

The doctor stood in the door with two loaves of our bread inder his arm and asked if they could have the recipe. He said ome more and Mother laughed high and tinkly like the wind himes and said she'd always wanted to play bridge, she'd just ever had anyone offer to teach her and yes, she'd be glad to ive him the recipe.

She sent me the next day with the recipe which I put inder a stone for a moment while I helped Rudy untangle ather's fishing reel, which was tied to a kite. We couldn't fix t, so we buried the reel in the garden and when I got back, I tood and watched the wind flip the paper under the stone. Chen I saw Emily's bicycle lying in her driveway and I lifted he stone and let the recipe blow away. I told Mother the loctor's wife said she didn't have time to bake bread.

When Father came home for supper, Mother was banging ots on the stove and said that she wouldn't bother with bridge fter all, she had too much to do. Father said there was no rest or the wicked and Mother laughed, and her laughter was like ubbing two stones together.

The Rock Garden

I WAS one of four children who stood beneath the maple tree early one morning. We were on our way to school. Mika, our mother, had spit and licked and polished and we were fresh and as clean as was the day which smelled to me of lilacs. Above us, leaf buds, tight like babies' fists, began uncurling fingers one by one to the sun. It wasn't a day to argue. We stood beneath the tree looking down at a rock. The rock had appeared mysteriously overnight and we, like curious animals, sniffed and poked at it.

"I wonder where it came from," I said.

Truda, the third eldest, spoke. "It could have been a dog. A dog carried it in its mouth and dropped it."

Betty laughed at Truda and tickled the top of her head. "Silly."

I nudged the rock with my foot. It wouldn't budge and I was relieved, seeing in my mind the possibility of a garter snake curled beneath it, or thick slugs kissing the damp bottom of the rock with their sucky mouths.

I was the only black-haired child of the six Lafreniere children. My skin didn't blister and peel in the sun, but tanned to the colour of a netted gem potato, dusty and dry looking. My hair, straight and black, resembled Maurice's, my father's hair. I was the only child in our family who looked like a Lafreniere should look, fine-boned, tiny feet and hands, small black eyes. I was conscious of being different, and felt cocky and self-assured in this difference. "It looks like a rock," I said. "But it could be something else, you know. It could, for instance, be a fossilized dinosaur egg. It was dug up when they made the ring dike."

"Yes, it could be an egg," said the myopic Truda.

I could tell that Betty was stung by Truda's disloyalty; usually they were a team. "We'll be late for school," Betty said. "And then I'll get the blame for it. I'm the example." She gathered her books up from the grass and headed down the cinder-strewn driveway.

"If it's a dinosaur egg," Rudy said, always wanting to get to the truth of the matter, "then it might hatch, won't it? I think it will. And then it'll eat us up."

"It can't hatch," I told him. "It hasn't been fertilized." Put that in your pipe and smoke it, as my father would say. I took Truda and Rudy by the hand and led them down the dirt road where we traced our own footprints in the bottom of the deep ruts. Betty followed along behind us, neat and proper, never galloping, our perfect example.

After a time, we left the road and entered the coulee, a grassy dish of marshland that filled each spring with water which receded quickly, leaving behind twitch grass that grew waist-high, and spotted toads that leapt up before our feet.

"I am thee Count," a voice said in Draculan tones. "Let me bite your neck. Heh, heh, heh." Laurence Anderson's brown curly head parted the grasses as he stood up and came towards us. He carried a paper sack and wiped his palms against his white T-shirt, leaving behind grey smudges of something he'd been into.

"It's puke-face himself."

"Lureen!"

I knew Betty would tell Mother. Lureen swore, she'd say, her blue eyes wide with a pretended innocence. Lureen said: shit, piss and God. Exaggerating, because reciting the words was the only way Betty had the courage to do it too. And Mother would believe her because Betty was her favourite child. Betty had memorized one hundred Bible verses and won a trip to church summer camp. Our mother respected those who could do what she couldn't.

Girls don't swear, she often said.

But they do on Father's side of the family, I argued.

Well, I guess. What can you expect, she said. There are no ladies in your father's family. None that I know of. They're coarse and hard. They paint their nails. They walk around in their war paint looking as though they've dipped their fingers in someone's blood. You want to be like that? I knew nothing of my father's family except what my mother told me. But, yes, that sounded exciting.

Why don't girls swear? Because, Mother said when she didn't want to talk to us, just because. Because I say so. And then, exasperated, it gives boys the wrong impression, you know. That you aren't to be respected. That you're Fair Game. Like a female dog in heat.

What is Fair Game? I wondered, and imagined a prairie chicken flapping up from the grass in the coulee. I was twelve years old, I knew what the spring dance of the dogs meant and

I thought that she was coarse and hard for referring to it. But what was Fair Game?

Sometimes my mother would say, men, who needs them? In the same derogatory way she discussed my uncles' wives. She would say, Lureen, you would be "wery vise" to forget about boys until you have an education.

By education, Mother meant grade twelve, which, to me, seemed a preposterous length of time to wait for boys, an indication of her being so out of touch with reality, that her opinion couldn't be trusted. A person whose English was so faulty that they said, "wery vise," lost their credibility. Piss, shit and God are nothing to get excited about, my father would say with a laugh.

I began to hum because I knew it annoyed Laurence. "Twit," he said, not looking at me directly. He fell into step with Betty. "Wait until you see what I found," he said to her.

I wanted to fling mud at him. A solid blow to his shaggy head. Wham! It made me angry the way he followed Betty around when it was so obvious to me that I was better-looking. I watched as Laurence held open the paper bag and Betty looked inside it. Since Betty's new breasts, Mother's objections to their friendship had grown stronger. If I went to her and told her that they had met in the coulee, that would be that. But I wouldn't do that because I was beginning to use Betty's sins against her, to realize that there was something to my mother's admonition that sisters should be friends.

"What is it?" There was fear in Betty's voice. "Where did you find that awful thing?"

Laurence closed the bag quickly at the word "awful" and clutched it against his chest.

"I found it where they're digging," he said. "It's mine now. I'm going to keep it."

Betty looked frail and meek against the tall, sharp-bladed grasses. Her hair was wound about her head in a golden crown of tight braids which made her neck look thin, too thin to support so large a head. "But why would you want to?" she asked. "It looks real, like a real person's—"

"It is," said Laurence. "It's a human skull."

"But it must be wrong, you should get rid of it, bury it or something."

Let me look, I wanted to say, but they had joined themselves against me, turned their backs and were lost in their own conversation. I wanted to look inside the bag, force myself to touch, hold in my hands, whatever it was that frightened Betty, to show Laurence that he'd made a mistake in choosing Betty over me.

Weeks later, the lilacs had finished blooming and were just rust-coloured flecks on the ground, and now there were seven buff-coloured, pumpkin-sized rocks on the ground beneath the maple tree. Truda had wised up by then, and decided that the rocks weren't dinosaur eggs. "Maybe Mother laid them, like a chicken," she said once. That morning, when another stone had been added by mysterious circumstances to the growing mound of them beneath the rope swing, Truda called me over to examine the new rock and said, "Look at that, she laid another egg."

Rudy was there too. He was pumping fruitlessly on the rope swing, trying to gain some height, but his feet kept glancing off the stones, making the swing careen wildly, bringing his shins too close to the rough bark of the maple tree. "Damn," Rudy said. "I don't think it's fair that we can't use the swing."

"Do something," Truda pleaded, her heavy thick glasses slipping down her nose and her myopic grey eyes clouded and pleading.

I decided to do something about the stones. I marched into the house and faced my father who had his day off from the barbershop and was sprawled in the maroon easy chair with his bare feet propped up on the hassock. He hid behind a magazine so he wouldn't have to take note of the multi-coloured and malodorous piles of dirty laundry Mother sorted in the living and dining room every Monday.

Why do you have to do the laundry on my day off for God's sake, he complained. And I agreed fully, it was inconsiderate.

Because, she said. Just because I have to. Monday is wash-day. I can't help it if it also happens to be your day off.

Father looked at me overtop his *Game and Fish* magazine. "How should I know where the rocks came from? I'm not the chief cook and bottle washer around here." He tried to tease me from my seriousness. "Serious, serious," he'd say. "That's your mother's department." His small black eyes reflected light in a curious way, making him look as though he were about to burst into tears or laughter. I could never tell which.

"Why don't you ask your mother where the rocks came from? She should know."

Everything in the yard and the two-story frame house belonged absolutely to us, the children. Mother had always arranged everything according to the patterns of our play. So the rocks were encroaching on our territory. I went to the kitchen where she folded diapers at the table. The washing machine sloshed and chugged another load clean in the back porch. There were two stacks of diapers, Peter's and Sharon's, white unspotted flannel, smelling of the reedy wind that blew in from the coulee.

"What rocks?" Mother asked.

"You know. Under the swing. Those rocks."

"They're mine." Her voice snapped the sentence shut the same way her strong white teeth nipped at knots in laces. You could ask Father anything and get an interesting, amusing answer, but not Mother. She was as serious as a mousetrap.

"What are they for? We can't use the swing anymore."

"Swing, fling. You're too old anyway. And you don't really care about the others, you just want to stir up trouble. I know you." She flicked a diaper and folded it into the shape of a kite, triple folds for Peter, because a boy pees the front. "Anyway, you have the rest of the yard to do what you want."

"It's our yard."

"I beg your pardon?"

"You should give us a reason, at least. You should tell us what the rocks are for."

"I don't have to tell you anything, missy," she said. "You only want reasons so that you can argue."

The sun moved behind the clouds for a moment and the yellow kitchen walls lost their sheen as the shadow came and fell on Mother's face, making her deeply set hazel eyes sink even further back into their bony sockets.

"O Lord," she said. "Please don't let it rain today."

"Why not?" I asked, grateful that she had been diverted from the tone of 'I beg your pardon.'

"You think I like mud from one end of this house to the other?"

The cloud passed and the room shone once again, but it seemed to me that pieces of the shadow lingered in her eyes. A creeping uneasiness made me close the screen door behind me gently.

That same evening as the garden arose silently from the black earth behind the chicken wire fence, I awoke to the sound of the latch on the screen door. I thought it was Father coming home from the hotel. But instead of my father's heavy step in the kitchen, there were light footsteps on the sidewalk at the side of the house and then silence. I looked out across the coulee and imagined Laurence crouching in the tall weeds, like a prairie chicken about to spring up. The moon was a silver disc, licked and pressed onto a black broadcloth sky.

The night breezes fanned the tops of the grass in the coulee and sounded like the whispering of a single voice.

Let me bite your neck.

Mother stepped out from beneath the maple tree and crossed the yard to the driveway. She left the yard and walked down the centre of the road, head bent into the darkness. The moon revealed the fish-white muscles in her calves. Mother's knotted tanned arms, her strong back, the muscles in her legs made her look chunky and shorter than she really was. She could carry a hundred-pound sack of flour in her arms. A dog barked in the distance and Mother vanished into the inky darkness. I knelt beside the window to wait.

When I awoke, my knees were stiff from kneeling. The wind had fallen. From Main Street came the insistent toot of a car horn. At the end of the street there was another sound. The sound was a needle-thin one, yet musical, like a violin being plucked instead of bowed. A blotted figure emerged from the darkness and gradually came to the light. The plucking sound was Mother's voice raised softly in a song. She came to the light. Her hair was unwound and flowed in a brown cascade of ripples across her shoulders. She carried a rock in her arms. She turned in at the driveway beneath the window. Still singing lightly, she strode across the yard and laid the stone gently down among the others.

Weeks later, the sweet peas had climbed to their glory on the chicken wire fence surrounding the garden and the bees droned above the profusion of pea blossoms. I was behind the sweet peas, hoeing the potato patch. I was unhappy. Laurence had put his hand on Betty's breast in the coulee. They thought I hadn't seen. I hadn't told anyone although I was burning with the desire to do so. I heard a noise and looked up. Laurence was there, behind the tree out of sight, should anyone look out the window. He played with his knife. He held the blade at the end and then flung it, making the blade turn once in mid-air before it cut into the tree.

"That's easy," I said. "I can do that." I'd dropped the hoe, come to watch.

"You think you're so tough," Laurence said.

"I don't think. I know I am."

"God, you make me sick." He bent to pick up the knife which had bounced off the bark and stuck into the ground.

I beat him to it, grabbed the knife before he'd had the chance to reach for it.

"Give it to me."

"Make me."

His hand was strong on my wrist, chapped and raw-looking like his mouth; it felt like sandpaper as he twisted my skin red. I felt tears forming. They were going to squirt forward onto my cheeks in a second and betray me if I didn't do something. I made a fist with my free hand, punched him hard in the middle of his dirty T-shirt. Woof, he said, sounding like a dog, and let go of me.

"Here's your stupid knife." I threw it onto the rock pile. My wrist ached. I walked away from him rapidly and entered the house. I could hear Mother moving about in the rooms upstairs.

"If you've got nothing better to do, you could give me a hand," she said.

I sat cross-legged on the floor beside the bed as Mother changed the linens. I let my head drop so that my hair fell forward and hid my face. The effect I hoped to achieve was a look of despair or dejection.

"What is it?"

It worked. I sighed deeply.

"Well, out with it."

"I don't know—it's just that he follows her around. As though she were a bitch in heat. We can never go anywhere without him."

"What did you say?"

"I said, I'm fed up. Everywhere we go, there he is. It's like we're Fair Game."

The colour fled from Mother's cheeks. "Who's following you around?"

"Laurence. He's here again. And yesterday, when I went to school I saw him and Betty. He—they were necking."

Mother's shoulders sagged. She dropped a sheet and rushed over to the bedroom window. "Oh, this is no good," she said. "I don't like the sound of this at all."

She clattered down the stairs and then the front door rattled on its hinges. I got up from the floor and went over to the window and stood looking down at Laurence and Betty. I saw Mother run across the yard toward them. She hopped from foot to foot when she reached the pile of rocks.

"But Mother," Betty protested. "He's just fixing the swing. He's moving the ropes up so the little ones can use it."

"I'll fix him. Just you let him come around again and I'll fix him." Mother turned to Betty and shook her finger. "Really, you'd think you'd have more pride." She sputtered and glanced up at the bedroom window where I watched. "Don't you want more than that for yourself?"

I parted the curtains and smiled at the sight of Laurence retreating, edging backwards from the yard.

"Wait," Mother said and held out her hand. "Give me your knife."

Laurence removed it from its leather sheath. The blade shone as it crossed the space between them. She grabbed it from him and, teetering up the stony mound of rocks beneath the tree, she cut through the ropes of the swing with saw-like motions. Betty ran into the house with her hands covering her face.

I saw the tanned V at Mother's throat rising and falling rapidly as she stood looking down the road where Laurence had gone and then back at the house. And then, as though she had come to some decision, she strode over to the icehouse and returned moments later pushing the wheelbarrow, which held a pail of whitewash and a paint brush. Betty rushed into the bedroom and threw herself onto the bed, crying loudly.

Mother stood beneath the maple tree with her hands on her hips. "Alright," she said loudly. "Alright, okay. You can't change a thing. No amount of harping will change anything. They'll do what they want to do in the end anyway. I'm butting my head against a stone wall." She pried open the pail of whitewash. "Don't take my advice. See what you get in the end." She stirred the thick paint and then dipped the brush into it. "Life is too short to butt your head against a stone wall." She began to paint a large rock a brilliant white. "And what do you get for it? Let them learn the hard way." She continued to complain bitterly as she finished painting the rock and set it aside. She rolled another stone down from the pile and began to paint it also.

An hour passed. Betty came to the window to watch what was happening below. We heard Peter the baby down in the kitchen banging impatiently on the tray of the highchair and the clatter of pots as Sharon amused herself in the cupboards. Mother continued to paint rock after rock and to place them into a large circle. I sent Truda and Rudy outside to make polite restrained overtures at conversation in order to jar Mother from her strange behaviour, but her sour expression sent them scurrying back into the house.

At a quarter to twelve, Father came walking up the sidewalk for his lunch. He stood waiting as Mother wheeled a load of dirt through the garden towards him.

"It's a funny time to start that job," he said, glancing at his watch.

"It's now or never."

Father shrugged. "Suits me. But what's for lunch?"

Mother looked up angrily. "Why don't you have a look?"

He came back out minutes later. "There's nothing prepared," he said, sounding injured and puzzled.

"I know."

"Why not?"

"Because," she said quietly and then once again, louder, "because. Just because. I don't know why. I'm tired of answering stupid questions. Make your own lunch."

"Listen here," Father said, his voice rising above its accustomed gentle tone. "The babies are in there alone. Their diapers are dripping."

"And does that bother you?"

"Of course, what do you think? Something could happen to them."

Mother grunted as the wheelbarrow tilted suddenly from her grasp and fell onto its side. "Well, change them then," she said. "They're your babies too."

"What's the matter?" he asked, lowering his voice. "Is it—are you in the family way?"

Mother stopped shovelling and looked him straight in the eye. "Yes. I'm always in the family way. And I'm tired. I'm tired of being a mother."

What? Tired of being a mother? It was an astounding thought. In the same way I grew tired of playing 7-up against the house, or sick of my best friend, so that I picked a fight in order to cut myself off from her, Mother was tired of us, her children?

Father turned from her in disgust. "Is that all?" he said. "Who doesn't get tired? What if I should say the same thing, eh? Where would you be?"

Absolutely, I agreed, where would you be without him? Where would any of us be?

"I would change places with you in a flash. You stay home, I'll go to work."

Father edged away from her. I had to do something. I knocked on the windowpane. "We're hungry," I said, reminding them both of their parental duties.

He looked up, startled. "What do you expect me to do about it?"

"Peter needs a bottle."

"I don't know what's going on here," Father said. "But I do know that I've got five heads waiting to be cut. So I'm going to grab a bite to eat at the hotel and then I'm going to get back to work. Somebody's got to work around here," he said loudly, for Mother's benefit.

"Oh, you're useless," she said. "You can go to the hotel. You couldn't look after a dog."

Father stared at her, shocked, and then retreated quickly.

"That's not fair," I said to my sister, "she's always so bloody unfair to him." Father had all the money. In case of marital breakdown, I wanted to be where the money was. So my sympathies in any of their arguments rested with him.

"I wouldn't know what's fair," Betty said. "Someone has to look after the kids today and I guess that leaves me." She went downstairs.

The sun passed centre sky and the birds stopped singing. I nibbled at the sandwich Betty had brought to me, but my stomach was tight and the food tasted flat. So, Mother was tired of being a mother, eh? The idea was like a thunderstorm. I was unsettled by the sound of it. I didn't know how she could be so selfish.

Wet stains spread across my mother's back and from beneath her armpits, as she began to form a smaller circle of rocks on top of the larger one. Her hair was pasted in strands against her white neck. She looked to me like a sweaty, irritable child. Back and forth she went, scooping up the black dirt, wheeling it across the yard to the tree, dumping it, shovelling it into place, raking it smooth, back and forth, with a bulldog determination. And then, on one of her trips, she stumbled, broke her stride and fell beneath the weight of the dirt in the wheelbarrow. She landed flat on her back. She looked like a beetle squirming to right itself. The more she floundered, the more exposed she became. Her blue cotton shift worked upwards, baring her thighs and then the white cotton v of her crotch.

My breath caught in my throat at the sight of my mother sprawled on the ground, at the sight of her vulnerability, that cotton mound between her legs.

She struggled upright, brushed dirt from her legs, her dress. I urged her to come inside. I wanted her to give up this silly project, wash her hands, or take up the broom and become a mother again. But she didn't. When she'd finished brushing herself off, she took up the handles of the wheelbarrow and began to fill in the second circle with earth.

She was forming the last, smallest circle when the sun began its falling behind the house, casting long pale shadows across the grass. Betty stood in the doorway of the bedroom with diaper pins in her mouth and a towel draped over her shoulder.

"I need a hand," she said.

"It's not our job," I said. "It's her job. Let her come and do it. She doesn't care if we starve, she only cares about herself." But my heart wasn't in it.

Betty threw the towel at me. "There's enough babies around here already without you becoming one too. Help me get them washed and into bed."

Together we bathed the children and put them into bed. We took turns reading stories to them to take their minds off their mother who wouldn't come inside and be a mother.

I listened to Betty's flat monotone voice reading, wooing the babies to sleep. Part of what happened was my fault. If I hadn't told on my sister, none of this would have happened. I would make tea, arrange a tray of food and lure her back inside. I might even begin to help around the house. Maybe finish changing the linens on the bed. Might not complain when asked to wipe the dishes.

I heard the door of the icehouse being closed. I crept to the window, looked down to see Mother scraping her shoes on the footscraper. I beckoned Truda and Rudy from the bed. They tiptoed to the window. I instructed them to say goodnight. I arranged them side by side. They cleared their throats. One, two, three—now.

"Goodnight Mother."

She'd have to answer. She'd say, "Don't let the bed bugs bite. And then they would reply, "Oh no, we'll hit them black and blue with our shoes." We waited. No answer. I nudged them again. "Goodnight," they called once more. Their voices, clear in the moisture-laden air, were fruity and sweet.

Still no answer.

The screen door flapped shut. There was a long silent time. Then we heard the kitchen chair creaking beneath her weight and then the sound of her shoes dropping one after the other to the floor.

I'll memorize Bible verses, I vowed silently. I'll follow Betty's example. Then I stopped breathing, listened, as there came another sound from below. It was the dry swishing sound of the broom being swept briskly across the kitchen floor.

I began to breathe once again. "She's back. Listen, she's sweeping the floor." I sat down beside Betty who had gathered her knees up and rocked back and forth in the centre of the bed.

My body felt weak, overpowered by the flooding of relief. The crisis was over. "I'll make tea," I said, "if you help me get together a plate of food for her."

"Are you crazy?" Betty said. "After what she did to Laurence? You go ahead and do that if you want to, but I couldn't care less."

I went back to the window to think about this new development. The rock garden glowed strangely in the falling light.

Beside it on the ground were the ropes from our swing, curled like two large question marks. The rocks' pink glow dimmed slowly to a violet and then at last, a dull grey. My resolutions faded gently. Oh well, I told myself, she's used to making her own tea anyway. If I offered to make it, the shock would kill her.

"I know what you mean," I said. "What she did to Laurence was awful. I almost died. And it wasn't fair, either. He was only trying to help. She's so unfair."

"She's a witch," Betty, my example, said, "a frigging witch."

The first of the whispering sounds swept in from the coulee, gently puffing the curtains in and out like a frog's throat. I felt a slight chill. The sounds brought with them mystery, uncertainty.

Let me bite your neck.

I knew my mother had some of the answers to the mysteries. But the pull of an alliance between sisters was stronger. It was better than being on your own with a person who could suddenly grow tired of being your mother.

"Piss, shit and God," I said. "A mean witch." I stepped out and away from my mother. Suddenly, I was afraid.

Night Travellers

"WHEN A woman has intercourse," Mika told herself, "she thinks of what might happen." She climbed in the night the hill that led away from the river and James. She travelled in a black and white landscape because it was void of details that would have demanded her attention. And the night was also a cover. Above, the starlit summer sky served only to make God seem more remote, withdrawn. As she walked, she took comfort in the sound of the frogs in the moist ditches on either side of the road, the call of an owl hunting in the park below.

Men, she was certain, thinking of both James and Maurice, didn't think of such things as a seed piercing another seed and a baby growing instantly, latching itself fast to the sides of her life. Men were inside themselves when they shot their juices. It was just another trick that God played, to keep the babies coming. Replenish the earth. Well—she was doing her job.

She reached the top of the hill and then she stooped slightly, giving in to the weight of a stone which she cradled close to her breasts. If Maurice should ever think to ask, she would be able to say, "I was out gathering rocks for my rock garden. It's the only time I can go, when the children are sleeping." And she would still be telling the truth.

She stopped to catch her breath and turned to look back at the park beside the river. Lot's wife looking back with longing towards a forbidden city. But unlike Lot's wife, she did not become a pillar of salt. From among the trees in the park, light shone out from the tiny window in James's bunkhouse. He had turned on the lantern. Pride made her wish that he would have stood for a few decent moments and watched while she climbed the hill. For this reason she'd kept her back straight until she was certain he couldn't see her anymore. But already, he was stretched out, lost in one of the many books he kept on the floor beside the cot. What did she expect? That had been their agreement, not to look for anything from each other. She had Maurice and the children. He had his dream of voyages in a sailboat.

At the top of the hill, the road stretched broad and straight, one half mile to the centre of town. She could see lights as cars on Main Street headed in and swiftly out of town. She passed by the grove of fruit trees that surrounded her parents' garden. The scent of ripe fruit carried across the road and she thought of the apples her mother had given to her, baskets of them, in the bottom of the cupboard. Her parents' white cottage stood beyond the garden in the darkness. I'm sorry, she said. I forgot about the apples. But with the children my hands are already full. She thought of the children, round cheeked and flushed with their dreams and her step quickened.

Beyond the ditch, there was a sudden rustling sound, like an animal rising up quickly. Mika, startled, stood still and listened. A dark figure stepped from the cover of the fruit trees onto the path that joined the cottage to the road.

"Who's there?" She heard movement, fabric rubbing against fabric. A dry cough. "Papa, is that you?"

Her father came forward in the darkness. Relief made her knees weak.

"Liebe, Mika. I was hoping, but I knew in my heart it was you."

Knew it was me, what? What did he know? "What are you doing up so late?" she asked instead. "The night air isn't good for your lungs."

"When one of my children is in trouble, I don't worry about such things."

"What's this, trouble?" she asked. She felt her heart jump against the stone she clutched tightly to her breast. As he turned towards her, he was illuminated by the moon and she saw that he'd pulled his pants on over his night clothes. His shirt lay open, exposing the onion-like skin on his chest to the cool breeze. She saw concern for her in the deep lines in his face. If only he would use anger, it would be easier to oppose him.

"Nah, you know of what I speak. I've seen your coming and going. I've seen him. I'm ashamed for you."

"What you've seen is me gathering rocks for a rock garden." She held up the stone. "I gather them from beneath the bridge."

"Mika." There was sorrow in his voice.

It was the same tone of voice he'd used on her all her life. It made her change her course of action because she didn't want to be responsible for his sorrow. It was the same thing with Maurice. Peace at all costs. Maurice had forced himself on her and she'd forgiven him because of an offer to build a new window in the kitchen. She hated that about herself.

"So, you've seen my coming and going and you're ashamed for me. I'm not."

He blocked her path. "Come to tne house. We should talk and—"

She pushed around him and began to walk away. Talk? Talk about Maurice and his black night moods? About another baby coming in a house full of babies? No, we will talk about my responsibilities instead.

"Have you travelled that far then," she heard him call after her, "that you can now make excuses for your behaviour? What am I to tell the elders at church?"

Before her, silhouetted against the sky, the flutter of wedge-shaped wings, two bats feeding on insects. They would become entangled in her hair. She heard his light step on the road and then he walked beside her. "Why should you tell them anything?" she asked. "It's none of their concern. What I do is my own business."

"We're a community," he said. "People united by our belief, like a family. When one member hurts, the whole family suffers."

"A family. I'm not part of that family," Mika said. "I don't belong anywhere."

"How can you say that? The women welcome you into their homes. They pray for you."

"Oh, they welcome me, alright. I'm to be pitied, prayed for. It gives them something to do."

They walked for a few moments without speaking. He pulled at his thick white mustache, the way he did when he was deep in thought. She stopped, turned to him. "Look, Papa. You know they don't accept Maurice. Even if he wanted to go, they don't invite him into their homes. They don't really accept me, either. So, if you feel it's important to tell the elders, tell them. I don't care."

The bats—their flight was a dance, a sudden dipping, a flutter, a smooth glide and they swerved back in among the trees. Gone. She walked faster. "The children are alone," she said.

"Oh, so you think of the children at least?" he said.

"Of course I think of them. I need something for myself too."

He put his large cool hand on her arm and drew her to the side of the road. His sun-tinged complexion had paled and there was fear in his eyes. "But not this," he said. "Not this. What are you saying? You need to ask God to forgive you. The wages of sin is death."

Always, Bible verses, given in love but becoming brick walls, erected swiftly in her path. The hair on her arms and neck prickled. "Papa," she said. "It's my sin and it's my death. Leave me be." She lifted the stone up and away from her breast and slammed it into the ground. She turned from him quickly and ran with her hands pressed against her stomach.

She undressed quickly, her heart still pounding, and listened to their sounds, the children, breathing all through the house. She'd stood first in one doorway, listening for them, then in another, and finally she'd bent over the baby in the crib at the foot of her bed. She'd felt for him in the dark, found a moist lump beneath the blankets. She'd changed his diaper without awaking him. Maurice was not home. He was still at the hotel. She waited for her heart to be still so that she could sleep. She rubbed her stomach gently. What would it be, she wondered, this one that she carried with her to James? Would it be touched or bent in any way by her anger? Below, a door opened. She stiffened, then rolled over and faced the wall as Maurice came up the stairs.

"What are you thinking?" James asked.

Mika swung her legs over the side of the cot and sat up. Her feet rested in a trapezoid of moonlight which shone through the small window of the bunkhouse. She'd been half-listening to James telling her about some one person he knew who had never let him down. His voice rose and fell in its strange British accent and she was able to think above it. Through the other small window at the end of the bunkhouse, she could see her parents' cottage, a white sentinel on a hill. It was in darkness once again, but she was certain her father's white face looked out from behind the lace curtains.

"Oh, I'm not thinking about any one thing in particular." But all day she'd been wondering, how could you be forgiven by God for something you'd done if you weren't sorry you'd done it?

He rose up on his elbow and ran his hand along her arm. The smell of the bunkhouse was his smell, faintly like nutmeg, the warmth of sun trapped in weathered grey planks and it was also the smell of the other men who had slept there; the men who had come to town as James had after the flood to help clean and rebuild it. She put her hand overtop his.

"God, you're beautiful," he said.

"Don't say that."

"What, not say you're beautiful?" He laughed and sat up beside her. He reached for his cigarettes on the windowsill. "You're a strange one."

He was tired of listening to himself talk and had drawn her in by saying, "You're beautiful." In the beginning, he'd pranced around her, so obviously delighted that he'd charmed her into coming away from the riverbank with him, through the park to this bunkhouse. He'd followed her about, picking up the clothing she'd shed, hanging it over a chair so she wouldn't look rumpled when she left. He was a meticulous lovemaker. He began by kissing the bottoms of her feet, the backs of her knees, her belly, causing the swing of the pendulum inside her to pause for several seconds at midpoint, so that she was neither being repelled nor attracted but suspended and still.

"Why don't you want me to tell you that you're beautiful?" James asked.

Because she didn't think she was beautiful. There was nothing beautiful about a person who would come home swollen and moist from lovemaking into the bed of another man. But what Maurice had done was not beautiful either. Two wrongs don't make a right, she'd instruct her own children.

"No, what I meant was, don't say God. Don't bring God into this."

Their thighs touched as they sat on the edge of the cot and she was amazed at how quickly she had become accustomed to the touch and smell of another man. The flare of his match revealed his exquisitely ugly nose. It was a fleshy hook pitted with blackheads. His chin and the skin around his mouth was deeply scarred by acne. You're so ugly, she'd once told him. She'd watched for evidence of injury, a faltering of his tremendous self-confidence. He'd laughed at her attempt, saw through it. She saw him daily as he walked past the house and he was always in a hurry, loose-jointed and thin, moving towards some vision he had of himself and his future.

He held the lit cigarette up to his watch. "Shouldn't you think about heading back? It's almost twelve."

"I've still got time."

He got up from the cot and his tanned chest moved into the trapezoid of light and then his buttocks, pinched together, muscular as he walked to the table beneath the window. He gathered up her hairpins and dropped them into her lap. He never forgot. He made certain each time that she left exactly as she'd come. She scooped the pins up and put them into the pocket of her dress.

"Don't you think you should fix your hair?"

"It's alright. Maurice is never home before I am."

He leaned over her, kissed her forehead. He slipped his hand inside her unbuttoned dress and fondled her. "I love your breasts. I think that's what I'll miss the most about Canada, your beautiful sexy breasts."

She put her arms about his neck and drew him down on on top of her. "Once I'm gone," he said into her neck, "if we ever meet again, it will be chance. You know that, don't you?"

"Yes." In another month he wouldn't want her anyway. Already she could feel the baby between them. She listened to the sound of his heart pushing against her chest. The wind had fallen and the silence in the park was complete, the river still. The moment passed. She fingered the hair pins in her pocket. She pulled them loose and scattered them into the folds of his blanket. He'd find them tomorrow. When he was making his bed, tight corners, planning his day, his mind leaping forward to the next event, he'd find her pins and he'd think of her for one second. She knew he wouldn't think of her longer than that, or wonder what she might be doing at that moment or try and recall her features as she did his; she even longed for the sight of his lanky body, his brown trousers flapping loosely about his ankles, the funny way he walked, arms swinging, leading with his ugly nose. I thought of you today, he'd said once. And I got this enormous stiff prick. I think of you too. She couldn't say, I love you.

"You'd better go," he said. "Before I change my mind and keep you here with me all night."

She pushed him from her, sat up and buttoned her dress. She used his comb and began combing her hair which was tangled and damp with sweat. The comb seemed to contain some residue of his energy, a reminder of the range of feelings she'd experienced only thirty minutes before. James got up, walked to the door and she followed him. He stood naked on the step. She gave him the comb. He plucked her dark hairs from its teeth and let the breeze catch them away. Above them, the stars were brilliant and clear. "Will you come tomorrow?" he asked.

"I don't know. If I can, I will."

"Try." He took her hand in his. He pressed the hairpins into her hand. "You've forgotten these."

Mika walked up the hill away from the park, the river, James. She heard nothing of the sounds of the night, the singing of insects, the owl hunting, nor did she see the phosphorus glow of fireflies among the tall grasses in the ditch. She was listening to the sound of her feet on the road, her heart beating, her breath labouring slightly as she climbed the hill and her thoughts. How could she be forgiven by God and brought to a state of serenity and continue to see James at the same time?

When she reached the top of the hill, her father waited on the path, pacing back and forth, swishing mosquitoes from his arms with a switch of leaves. Mika walked faster so that he would know she had no intention of stopping. He ceased pacing. She lifted her head and strode by him. She felt the sting of leaves on her legs. She stopped suddenly, her breath caught in her throat, and fought back anger. He threw the switch aside.

"Where is the stone you've been searching for tonight?" he asked.

"I have nothing to say. You can't make me argue with you. If you want to argue, then do it with yourself." Her voice did not betray her anger. She still felt the biting edge of the leaves on her skin. She walked away swiftly, and then faster until she was running from him. Her breath became tight and then a spot of fire burned in her centre. But she wouldn't stop running until she was home, safe, behind the door.

She sat at the kitchen table and pressed her face against the cool arborite. To be alone for once, just to be left alone. She listened to a fly buzzing against a window. The wind in the kitchen curtain swept against the potted plant. Water dripped into the sink. Something sticky against her arms — she sat up and frowned as her hand met toast crumbs and smears of jam left behind by one of the children. Her legs felt weak as she went over to the sink to stop the dripping of water and to get a cloth to wash the table. She reached to turn the light on above the sink and saw through the window her father entering the yard. She stood with her hands pressed to her face and waited. She wouldn't answer the door and he might think that she was upstairs, sleeping.

His light touch on the door, a gentle knock and — silence. Above her, the sound of electricity in the clock. He coughed twice. She could see him fumbling for his pocket, to spit his blood-flecked mucus into a handkerchief.

"Mika, I know you're there. Mika, open the door."

It wasn't locked, but she knew he wouldn't come in unless she opened it.

"You're causing much sorrow," he said. "Your mother has been crying most of the day."

Crying over children is a waste of time, Mika thought. In the end, they do what they want.

"She says for me to tell you, think of eternity."

The anger erupted. She stepped towards the closed door. "Eternity? Eternity? Papa, I've spent all my life preparing for eternity. No one tells me how to live each day. Right here, where I am."

She heard him sigh. "But when you think of it, we're here for such a little time when you consider all of eternity," he said.

"Yes, and it's my little time. Mine. Not yours."

He didn't speak for a few moments. She held her breath. She waited for him to leave. She sensed his wretched disappointment in her, his fading spirit. I can't help that, she told herself.

"Mika, one thing," he said. His voice was barely more than a whisper. "There's something wrong with your thinking. If we could just talk. I'm not well. I need to know before I —" He broke off and began to cough.

Before I die. She finished the sentence for him. She turned her back to the door and pressed her knuckles into her teeth and bit into them. Anger rose and grew until her fists were free and raised up. That he would try to use his illness against her. It's my life, she told herself. It's my life.

"Go away," she cried. She faced the door once again and stamped her foot. "Go away." She would tear the curtains from the windows, upset chairs, bring all the children running to stare at her anger. She would let them see what had been done to her, she would tell them, it's my life. She would—she gasped. A sharp kick in her belly, then a fluttering of a limb against her walls. Another movement, a sliding downward, a memory drawing her inside instantly like a flick of a knuckle against her temple. The baby. Like all the others asleep in the rooms upstairs, it travelled with her.

"Mika, please. I care for you."

She opened the door and stood before him, head bent and arms hanging by her sides. They faced each other. His shoulders sagged beneath his thin shirt. "Come in," she said. "I'll lend you one of Maurice's sweaters." She began to cry.

He stepped inside quickly and put his hand on her shoulder. "Yes, yes," he said. "That's it. You must cry over what you've done. It's the beginning of healing. God loves a meek and contrite heart."

She leaned into him, felt the sharpness of his rib cage beneath her arms. I cry because I can't have what I want. He's going away soon. I am meek and contrite because he doesn't want anything more than just a fleeting small part of what I am. I am filled with sorrow because I know myself too well. If I could have him, I wouldn't want him.

"It's over," he said. "You won't go and see that man again."

She heard the rasping sound of fluids in his chest. She loved him.

"No, I won't see him anymore."

She turned her face against his chest and stared into the night beyond him. She felt empty, barren, but at peace. In the garden, a bright glow flared suddenly and she thought, it's a cigarette. But the glow rose and fell among the vegetation and then became bead-shaped, blue, brighter, her desire riding the night up and up in a wide arc, soaring across the garden into the branches of thick trees. A firefly, Mika thought. And she watched it until it vanished.

Flowers for
Weddings and Funerals

MY OMAH supplies flowers for weddings and funerals. In winter, the flowers come from the greenhouse she keeps warm with a woodstove as long as she can; and then the potted begonias and asters are moved to the house and line the shelves in front of the large triple-pane window she had installed when Opah died so that she could carry on the tradition of flowers for weddings and for funerals. She has no telephone. Telephones are the devil's temptation to gossip and her God admonishes widows to beware of that exact thing.

And so I am the messenger. I bring requests to her, riding my bicycle along the dirt road to her cottage that stands water-marked beneath its whitewash because it so foolishly nestles too close to the Red River.

A dozen or two glads please. the note says. The bride has chosen coral for the colour of her wedding and Omah adds a

few white ones because she says that white is important at a
wedding. She does not charge for this service. It is unthinkable
to her to ask for money to do this thing which she loves.

She has studied carefully the long rows of blossoms to
find perfect ones with just the correct number of buds near
the top, and laid them gently on newspaper. She straightens
and absently brushes perspiration from her brow. She frowns
at the plum tree in the corner of the garden where the flies
hover in the heat waves. Their buzzing sounds and the thick
humid air make me feel lazy. But she never seems to notice
the heat, and works tirelessly.

"In Russia," she says as she once more bends to her task,
"we made jam. Wild plum jam to put into fruit pockets and
platz." Her hands, brown and earth-stained, feel for the proper
place to cut into the last gladiolus stalk.

She gathers the stalks into the crook of her arm, coral
and white gladiola, large icy-looking petals that are beaded
with tears. Babies' tears, she told me long ago. Each convex
drop holds a perfectly shaped baby. The children of the world
who cry out to be born are the dew of the earth.

For a long time afterward, I imagined I could hear the
garden crying and when I told her this, she said it was true.
All of creation cries and groans, you just cannot hear it. But
God does.

Poor God. I squint at the sun because she has also said
He is Light and I have grown accustomed to the thought that
the sun is His eye. To have to face that every day. To have to
look down and see a perpetually twisting, writhing, crying
creation. The trees have arms uplifted, beseeching. Today I
am not sure I can believe it, the way everything hangs limp
and silent in the heat.

I follow her back to the house, thinking that perhaps
tonight, after the wedding, there will be one less dewdrop in
the morning.

"What now is a plum tree but a blessing to the red ants and flies only?" She mutters to herself and shakes dust from her feet before she enters the house. When she speaks her own language, her voice rises and falls like a butterfly on the wind as she smooths over the gutteral sounds. Unlike my mother, who does not grow gladiola or speak the language of her youth freely, but with square, harsh sounds, Omah makes a sonatina.

While I wait for her to come from the house, I search the ground beneath the tree to try to find out what offends her so greatly. I can see red ants crawling over sticky, pink pulp, studying the dynamics of moving one rotting plum.

"In Russia, we ate gophers and some people ate babies." I recall her words as I pedal back towards the town. The glads are in a pail of water inside my wire basket. Cool spikelets of flowers seemingly spread across my chest. Here I come. Here comes the bride, big, fat and wide. Where is the groom? Home washing diapers because the baby came too soon.

Laurence's version of that song reminds me that he is waiting for me at the river.

"Jesus Christ, wild plums, that's just what I need," Laurence says and begins pacing up and down across the baked river bank. His feet lift clay tiles as he paces and I squat waiting, feeling the nylon filament between my fingers, waiting for something other than the river's current to tug there at the end of it.

I am intrigued by the patterns the sun has baked into the river bank. Octagonal shapes spread down to the willows. How this happens, I don't know. But it reminds me of a picture I have seen in Omah's Bible or geography book, something old and ancient like the tile floor in a pharaoh's garden. It is recreated here by the sun on the banks of the Red River.

"What do you need plums for?"

"Can't you see," he says. "Wild plums are perfect to make wine."

I wonder at the tone of his voice when it is just the two of us fishing. He has told me two bobbers today instead of one and the depth of the stick must be screwed down into the muck just so. Only he can do it. And I never question as I would want to because I am grateful to him for the world he has opened up to me. If anyone should come and join us here, Laurence would silently gather his line in, wind it around the stick with precise movements that are meant to show his annoyance, but really are a cover for his sense of not belonging. He would move further down the bank or walk up the hill to the road and his bike. He would turn his back on me, the only friend he has.

I have loved you since grade three, my eyes keep telling him. You, with your lice crawling about your thickly matted hair. My father, being the town's barber, would know, Laurence. But I defied him and played with you anyway.

It is of no consequence to Laurence that daily our friendship drives wedges into my life. He stops pacing and stands in front of me, hands raised up like a preacher's hands.

"Wild plums make damned good wine. My old man has a recipe."

I turn over a clay tile and watch an earthworm scramble to bury itself, so that my smile will not show and twist down inside him.

Laurence's father works up north cutting timber. He would know about wild plum wine. Laurence's mother cooks at the hotel because his father seldom sends money home. Laurence's brother is in the navy and has a tattoo on his arm. I envy Laurence for the way he can take his time rolling cigarettes, never having to worry about someone who might sneak up and look over his shoulder. I find it hard to understand his kind of freedom. He will have the space and time to make his wine at leisure.

"Come with me." I give him my hand.

Omah bends over in the garden. Her only concession to
the summer's heat has been to roll her nylon stockings to her
ankles. They circle her legs in neat coils. Her instep is swollen,
mottled blue with broken blood vessels. She gathers tomatoes
in her apron.

Laurence hesitates. He stands away from us with his arms
folded across his chest as though he were bracing himself
against extreme cold.

"His mother could use the plums," I tell Omah. Her eyes
brighten and her tanned wrinkles spread outwards from her
smile. She half-runs like a goose to her house with her apron
bulging red fruit.

"See," I say to Laurence, "I told you she wouldn't mind."

When Omah returns with pails for picking, Laurence's
arms hang down by her sides.

"You tell your Mama," she says to Laurence, "that it takes
one cup of sugar to one cup of juice for the jelly." Her English is
broken and she looks like any peasant standing in her bedroom
slippers. She has hidden her beautiful white hair beneath a
kerchief.

She's not what you think, I want to tell Laurence and
erase that slight bit of derision from his mouth. Did you know
that in their village they were once very wealthy? My grandfather was a teacher. Not just a teacher, but he could have been
a professor here at a university.

But our heads are different. Laurence would not be
impressed. He has never asked me about myself. We are friends
on his territory only.

I beg Laurence silently not to swear in front of her. Her
freckled hands pluck fruit joyfully.

"In the old country, we didn't waste fruit. Not like here
where people let it fall to the ground and then go to the store
and buy what they could have made for themselves. And much
better too."

Laurence has sniffed out my uneasiness. "I like home made jelly," he says. "My mother makes good crabapple jelly

She studies him with renewed interest. When we each hav a pail full of the dust-covered fruit, she tops it with a cabbage an several of the largest unblemished tomatoes I have ever seer.

"Give my regards to your Mama," she says, as thoug some bond has been established because this woman make her own jelly.

We leave her standing at the edge of the road shieldin her eyes against the setting sun. She waves and I am so prou that I want to tell Laurence about the apple that is named fc her. She had experimented with crabapple trees for years an in recognition of her work, the experimental farm has give a new apple tree her name.

"What does she mean, give her regards?" Laurence asl and my intentions are lost in the explanation.

When we are well down the road and the pails begin t get heavy, we stop to rest. I sit beside the road and chew th tender end of a foxtail.

Laurence chooses the largest of the tomatoes carefull and then, his arm a wide arc, he smashes it against a tel phone pole.

I watch red juice dripping against the splintered gre wood. The sun is dying. It paints the water tower shades (gold. The killdeers call to each other as they pass as silhouette above the road. The crickets in the ditch speak to me of Omah greenhouse where they hide behind earthenware pots.

What does Laurence know of hauling pails of water fro: the river, bending and trailing moisture, row upon row? Wh; does he know of coaxing seedlings to grow or babies cryin from dewdrops beneath the eye of God?

I turn from him and walk with my face reflecting th fired sky and my dust-coated bare feet raising puffs of ange in the fine warm silt.

"Hey, where are you going?" Laurence calls to my retreating back. "Wait a minute. What did I do?"

The fleeing birds fill the silence with their cries and the night breezes begin to swoop down onto our heads.

She sits across from me, Bible opened on the grey arborite, cleaning her wire-framed glasses with a tiny linen handkerchief that she has prettied with blue cross-stitch flowers. She places them back on her nose and continues to read while I dunk pastry in tea and suck noisily to keep from concentrating.

"And so," she concludes, "God called His people to be separated from the heathen."

I can see children from the window, three of them, scooting down the hill to the river and I try not to think of Laurence. I haven't been with him since the day on the road, but I've seen him. He is not alone anymore. He has friends now, kids who are strange to me. They are the same ones who make me feel stupid about the way I run at recess so that I can be pitcher when we play scrub. I envy the easy way they can laugh at everything.

"Well, if it isn't Sparky," he said, giving me a new name and I liked it. Then he also gave me a showy kiss for them to see and laugh. I pushed against his chest and smelled something sticky like jam, but faintly sour at the same time. He was wearing a new jacket and had hammered silver studs into the back of it that spelled his name out across his shoulders. Gone is the mousey step of my Laurence.

Omah closes the book. The sun reflects off her glasses into my eyes. "And so," she says, "it is very clear. When God calls us to be separate, we must respond. With adulthood comes a responsibility."

There is so much blood and death in what she says that I feel as though I am choking. I can smell sulphur from smoking mountains and dust rising from feet that circle a golden calf.

With the teaching of these stories, changing from pleasant fairy tales of far away lands to this joyless search for meaning, her house has become a snare.

She pushes sugar cubes into my pocket. "You are a fine child," she says, "to visit your Omah. God will reward you in heaven."

The following Saturday, I walk a different way to her house, the way that brings me past the hotel, and I can see them as I pass by the window, pressed together all in one booth. They greet me as though they knew I would come. I squeeze in beside Laurence and listen with amazement to their fast-moving conversation. The jukebox swells with forbidden music. I can feel its beat in Laurence's thigh.

I laugh at things I don't understand and try not to think of my Omah who will have weak tea and sugar cookies set out on her white cloth. Her stained fingers will turn pages, contemplating what lesson to point out.

"I'm glad you're here," Laurence says, his lips speaking the old way to me. When he joins the conversation that leaps and jumps without direction from one person to another, his voice is changed. But he has taken my hand in his and covered it beneath the table. He laughs and spreads his plum breath across my face.

I can see Omah bending in the garden cutting flowers for weddings and funerals. I can see her rising to search the way I take and she will not find me there.

Judgement

IT WAS early morning when Mr. Thiessen died, and
wreaths of mist still hovered above the river in pockets, trapped
by the shadows of overhanging willow branches. His corpse lay
in the porch of a small white cottage. The cottage sat on the
edge of a town beside a road that led over a hill and down the
other side of it and came to an end in the river.

The expression frozen into the dead man's face was one of
determination. His nostrils were packed with wads of cotton,
making his nose his salient feature. When he'd been alive, his
predominating feature had been his eyes, blue as snow when
the sun has just dipped into the winter horizon. He always
seemed to be looking beyond into something that was invisible
to others. Even at the hotel in town, where he once walked late
at night to sweep rubble from the parlour floor, his blue eyes
contemplated a scene beyond the smoke-filled parlour, some-

thing amusing to make him stop sweeping and chuckle suddenly, or something sombre and dark which he would take to
the cottage with him to think about while he puttered in his
flower garden. But his pale blue eyes no longer looked into
the ridiculous or the profane. They were opened, staring up
at the rafters which were strung with bundles of dried basil
and sage leaves and spirals of flypaper thickly coated with the
husks of insects.

Outside the cottage, an old woman sat on a bench and
leaned against the narrow slats of the porch. The back of her
head was almost level with his where he lay inside on the
couch beneath the screened windows. She looked like a lizard
sunning itself in the early morning on a moss-covered rock.
She didn't wear her dentures and so her caved-in mouth made
her nose jut forward from her face and her chin recede into
her neck. She sat shapeless and colourless with her sun-spotted
hands idle in her lap. The narrow slats of the porch wall
pressed into the woman's fleshy back but she didn't notice. She
was listening to the wind passing through the screens in the
windows above her kerchiefed head. She thought that the
sound of it was not a hopeless sound. It was the same sound as
the river rushing along its course to its irrevocable end in a
larger body of water. The wind had come early that morning,
before the sun, and had drowned out the fluttering sound of
her husband's breath struggling to free itself of the liquids in
his lungs. She blinked rapidly and folded one pudgy, spotty
hand over top the other.

She scratched at her ankle with her slippered foot. The
town was so still that she could hear the humming of electricity
in the wires along the road and the sound of blood rushing in
her veins. Birds cried as they circled the air above the river.
Get up, she told herself. Put on your workboots and go into
the back garden and pull the potatoes. All summer she had
plucked beetles from the leaves and squashed them between

her fingers. She had banked the plants with mounds of black dirt. Now is the time to pull the potatoes, she thought and then she caught herself. What am I doing? My husband is dead and I think of potatoes. But the idea of work to be done was restful. Instead of jumping up and running to the potting shed to take the bushel baskets down from the wall, she would rest. There was still time to sit. The town hadn't begun to stir and the doctor had yet to come and administer the six o'clock injection of morphine. She had this time of grace before she needed to accept the finality of her husband's stiffening blue-white features.

She bent down and picked at a loose thread on her plaid slipper and watched with fascination as the chain stitching unravelled. She looked about for a place to put the unravelled thread. She gathered it between her fingers and rolled it into a ball. She leaned back against the porch and through the slits of her half-closed eyes, she watched the sun rise. It was a fireball that swept from north to south above the trees that lined the river bank below. Back and forth it wheeled. She sighed and ran her tongue across her shrunken gums to erase a sour taste that nestled there like the orange sprinkles of beetles' eggs on the underside of a potato leaf. If only Eve hadn't sinned, she thought. Then there would have been no beetles to squash between her fingers or weeds to be hacked away. Because of Eve, each time her monthly bleeding had stopped and she'd been pregnant, she'd faced that nine months with dread, longing for a way around the curse. But there was no path around the pain of childbirth. You had to go through it before you could experience relief. It was all part of the curse, she told herself, beetles attaching themselves to her potatoes, childbirth and the silence in the porch.

She stared unblinking at the fireball above the trees and rolled the thread between her thick fingers until it was moist. Then she let it drop to the ground. She bent over, searched the other slipper for a loose thread, found one and pulled. What was worse for her now, she wondered? Loose threads or twenty-eight jars of watermelon pickles?

She saw them suddenly, the jars lined up on the shelves in the cellar, side by side, shining with the inner glow of the pale pink fruit, jewel-like and perfect. Of all the times he had to choose to die, it would be this time when the cellar was full of preserves. Yesterday he'd asked her for a dill pickle and she'd refused because they weren't sour enough. What did it matter whether the pickles were sour enough or not? What did it matter? Watermelon pickles or not watermelon pickles? What does anything matter now, she asked, but felt saddened by the look of her slippers. The tongues had been loosened when she'd pulled at the threads. They made things too cheaply. She forced her plucking hands to lie still in her lap. What am I to do now? she asked herself. What am I going to do with twenty-eight jars of watermelon pickles? She recited them:

> two dozen peaches in heavy syrup
> three dozen quarts crabs
> two and a half pints pears
> fourteen jars plum jam with wax seals, seven with tops
> one dozen two-quart sealers dills

And I couldn't even give him one.

The fireball climbed higher in the sky. The sound of the wind changed. It carried within it another sound. It was the sound of dried corn stalks when her skirts brushed against them. It was the sound of a man's hoarse whisper, urgent.

"Anna."

"Yes, what is it?" she asked. She had always promised herself that if an angel should speak, she would say, here am I, Lord.

"Water. Please. I want a drink."

She rose from the bench slowly. She climbed the three stairs. She entered the porch and passed by the bed of the dead man without looking at him. She went over to the treadle sewing machine where there was a tumbler and a jug of water. She tried to lift the jug. Her hands were two spotted stones dangling uselessly from the ends of her arms. She knew her husband was dead. She'd pulled the plaid blanket up around his chin and felt the unyielding heaviness of his cold arms when she'd placed them beneath the blanket. Could it be grief that caused her to hear voices where there should be none?

"I can't lift the jug. You don't really need water, do you?" Dried leaves stirred on the windowsill where his potted plants were lined, now just brown stalks in hard earth, neglected because of his illness. It was as though her words had lifted the leaves into motion.

"Ahh," his voice was expelled slowly. "Why would I ask you for water if I didn't need it? I'm so very hot."

The snake of fear uncoiled in her chest. Hot. He was hot? "Where are you?" she asked. She had warned him and warned him. All through the long night she had read the Bible, first the Psalms and then the New Testament, and had come to the parable of Lazarus and the rich man, when the sun first sat upon the trees. Send Lazarus to touch the tip of my tongue, she had read. The flames torment me. For those who didn't believe in a real hell, this was the place they should look, she was going to tell him and then noticed the absence of his rattling breath. She'd set the Bible aside, gotten up swiftly and knelt beside him and listened. His nose had stopped bleeding and the cotton wads in his nostrils were stiff with dried blood.

All night long he'd plucked at the cotton with his nicotine fingers and his sin had glared in the early morning light as she knelt beside his cooling body. His stained fingers were evidence of his sin, his habit of slipping into the potting shed every hour to roll a cigarette. The indelible yellow stains were proof of his imperfection. Where are you, God had asked Adam and Adam had answered, I hid because I was afraid;

and that was what he'd done too, shutting himself away inside the potting shed to smoke his cigarettes, as though God couldn't see. She'd knelt and prayed that God could overlook this one thing, but she doubted that He would. She saw her husband's nosebleeds, his coughing and spitting of blood as judgement of guilt. She'd warned him every single day for sixty-two years that this could happen.

"Where I am is not your concern," he said.

"Just so. Don't blame me if you're hot. What more could I do? I bathed you every hour. Now tell me, what else before I go? The potatoes are ready for pulling."

He looked past her with his steady contemplative blue gaze. He looked into each far corner of the porch and then up at the dangling spirals of flypaper. "What else? A smoke. Mother, make me a cigarette."

She was beyond anger. There was an immense sadness flooding into every part of her large body. "The body is the temple of the Holy Spirit. You would defile it with nicotine, even now?"

He sighed. He closed his eyes. His mouth was cracked from his fever. He ran his tongue across his chapped lips. She wondered if she should dip a hanky into the jug and moisten his lips for him and then she remembered that he was dead and she was standing there talking to a dead man and he was answering her, which was as far as she was willing to go, because he was not an angel.

"I never told you this," he said after a short time.

She stopped breathing.

"Never mind. It doesn't really matter."

"What? What?"

"It's nothing. I was going to say something about the way you look. But it doesn't matter."

She looked down at herself. There was nothing wrong with her appearance. She felt comfortable in the shapeless dress. She dressed in the manner fitting for an older Christian woman. Nothing between mid-calf and the neck was revealed. She even wore heavy cotton stockings during the summer.

He was casting stones at her to draw attention away from his own wrong-doing. "I'm running here and I'm running there," she said. "You make yourself sick, I have the running around. I wonder what you would look like if you followed me through the day? And what else? I stayed up and prayed for you all night. The girls come every day and I do the cooking. I haven't had time to fix my hair for three days and so I wear the scarf."

"I didn't mean that."

"What then?"

"It doesn't matter."

"Say it."

"I meant that—oh, I don't know if after sixty years it helps to say anything about it, but—you're too fat."

"I?"

He nodded his silver head.

She slammed the porch door behind her. Her slippers smacked loudly against the stairs. She suddenly hated the colour green. He'd painted the bench she'd sat on and the platform that held the rain barrel on the south corner of the house facing the potting shed and the three steps leading into the porch, the same vivid green as the fruit trees. He had never asked her, what do you think of green? Do you think green would be a fair colour? He'd never asked her whether she thought fruit trees across the back of the garden were a good thing. The first thing she would do would be to walk into town to the hardware store and buy a can of paint. Grey or brown, or something the colour of a potato beetle. And who would have to bring in his glad bulbs for winter storage? She would. Even though her vegetable garden had been placed in the back field farthest from the rain barrel and beneath the fruit trees (wood ticks in spring and three part rows of corn lost to the shade of the fruit trees) and even though his flowers had gradually taken over half of the vegetable garden, she'd never complained. A continual dropping on a very rainy day and a contentious woman were alike, the Bible said, and that was not her sin, being quarrelsome. Not that it would have helped to complain. Complaining would have just sent him into his faraway expression more often or into the potting shed. She would bring his glad bulbs in and she would also bring in the potatoes.

She sat back down on the bench and let her hands fall into her lap. She half closed her eyes once again, lulled by the sound of the wind in the screens. Even so, she told herself. Watermelon pickles or not watermelon pickles, what does it matter? Once more she viewed the sun through half-closed eyes. It became a fireball that jiggled and darted off to the right. She felt the warmth of it in her broad cheeks. It filled up all of her eyes. If she could turn her head right around, the fireball would make a full circle around her. She turned her head as far as it would go. The fireball followed. She turned her head the other way and heard the clatter of clay pots knocking against each other in the potting shed.

"And listen here, Father," she said. "And not only that. I told you and told you it wasn't a good thing to feed that cat. It's back here again. It's knocking over your plants. And who's going to have to clean up that mess, I wonder?" Hah, let the cat reach above the door where he hid his papers and the tin of tobacco and let the cat form a cigarette for him. That was what tobacco was good for. It was good for animals only. Poison for stray cats. She searched about in her dress pocket and found a peppermint candy. She rolled it about her mouth. She felt some of the tension begin to leave her body as its sweetness was released and slid down the back of her throat.

"Mother. Oh Mother. Are you still there?"

"I am here."

"Make me a cigarette, Mother. Just this once."

"Never. I won't be a part of you willfully harming your body."

"But you do it yourself."

She withdrew the diminished peppermint from her mouth and examined it closely. "That's foolishness," she said and put the candy back into her mouth. "God gave us food. If we didn't eat, we'd die."

"You refuse to make me a cigarette?"

"I refuse." She wouldn't have that on her conscience. She'd never made it easy for him. She hadn't permitted him to smoke his weed in the house. She was positive that he had her to thank for his eighty-one years. I have fought the fight, she told herself, I have won the race.

"In this case, I must obey God rather than man," she said and smiled gently, a toothless innocent smile. She waited for him to reply but heard instead the sound of a car moving slowly up the road. Six o'clock already. The fireball danced crazily. She arranged her skirt to cover her knees. The doctor's car entered the lane slowly and came to a halt. He got out of the car and walked across the yard and stood in front of her.

"Look," she said, and pointed to her feet. "My slippers are coming apart. They make everything too cheaply in this country."

"Nothing lasts forever," the doctor said. "Tell me, did Mr. Thiessen have a good night?"

"A good night, yes."

He was short and squat, wide enough to block out her view of the sun. She didn't like this man because even though she had never seen him smoke a cigarette, or smelled tobacco on his clothing, she suspected that he did smoke because he'd never reprimanded her husband for smoking or advised him to stop.

"And how about you?" he asked. "How did it go yesterday? Did your daughters come over and help out?"

"They come over every day," she said. "It's a little extra work cooking meals for them. But I don't mind."

"It's unfortunate at a time like this, but we do have to eat, don't we?"

"That's what I told him. God intended that we should eat."

He shifted his black bag from one hand to the other. "Some more than others." Then he set the bag down on the bench beside her, opened it and took out the stethoscope. "I may as well have a look at you too, while I'm here."

"There's nothing the matter with me."

"Give me your arm, please."

She held up her arm. He felt for her pulse. He frowned. He placed the stethoscope against the pulse in the crook of her arm, listened for a few moments and put the instrument back into his bag. "I'm not fussy about the sound of that," he said. She caught a fleeting glimpse of the syringe of painkiller that he'd come to inject into her husband's thin veins.

"Well," the doctor said. "Tell you what. It might be a good idea to have one of your daughters bring you into the office for a check-up. Do you think you could arrange that?"

"The potatoes are ready for pulling."

"The potatoes. I suppose so. But couldn't you get someone to do it for you this year?"

She stared at him.

"Well, never mind. We can talk about it later. I'll just have a look in on Mr. Thiessen right now."

"He's in the porch."

She heard the sound of his feet as he walked up the three green stairs. She heard the porch door squeak as it opened and closed. Her time of grace was over. She got up from the bench to follow the doctor. She heard the sound of pottery breaking in the potting shed.

That cat. She would have to go and chase that animal away before it broke every last one of her husband's pots. Why didn he think of those things? He fed the cat and left her to take care of the consequences. She took the broom down from its clasp on the wall beside the rain barrel. It was the outside broom, used to sweep dust and snow from shoes and for chasing animals. She raised the broom and walked lightly along the pathway to the potting shed. She was looking at the bottom of the door for the cat to come scooting out and then she would lower the broom. She saw her husband's shoes first. He was wearing his brown walking boots. Then her eyes travelled up the length of him until his blue eyes looked straight into her own.

"You! I thought it was a cat."

He'd pulled the cotton wads from his nostrils and his nose was back to its normal size. He wore his tweed cap low onto his forehead and his black serge jacket, the one he wore when he went to work at the hotel, was buttoned neatly. He clutched two earthenware pots, one inside the other, to his chest.

"Don't worry," he said finally. "I cleaned up the mess."

She lowered the broom and stepped to one side as he pushed past her on the narrow path. She caught a glimpse of a flash of yellow inside the pot which he held to his chest. It was his tobacco tin. He'd hidden his tobacco and papers down inside the earthenware pot.

"What are you doing? Where are you going with that?"

He walked away quickly, looking straight ahead. He passed by the green bench, strode jauntily down the lane to the dirt road.

"Father, wait. Leave the tobacco behind. Someone might see you." She followed him but the distance between them widened. She began to trot. What would people think if they saw him? She panted with the effort to keep up. The sound of her running pounded thickly inside her head. He was leaving her behind. "Wait for me. I want to come," she called one last time. But she knew it was useless. Once he'd made up his mind, there was no use talking. She sat down heavily on the bench and wiped perspiration from her forehead. He walked swiftly down the road to the bottom of the hill where the road flattened out towards the river.

He hesitated at the edge of the river and then turned around. He shielded his eyes with his hands. "Look here," he called to her. "I'm not coming back, so don't think that I am, because I'm not."

Tears burst and ran across her tanned broad cheeks. "And who is going to bring in your glad bulbs for winter?" she asked, hoping wildly to sway him with his beloved flowers. "I can't. The doctor says that maybe I should get someone to pull the potatoes."

He waved her question away. "Where I'm going there are enough flowers to go around and I will have my own mansion, white, with a flat roof like the houses in Mexico." He turned his back to her, faced the river and vanished. In the shadowy pockets along the riverbank, the wreaths of mist uncurled and evaporated in the sun. A crayfish scuttled along the muddy river bottom sending a swirl of yellow bubbles to break at the surface.

She felt the seconds fleeing from her. She had to do something, but what? What to do now that she was a widow? What would she do with ruined slippers and twenty-eight jars of watermelon pickles? She heard footsteps as the doctor descended the three stairs.

"He's dead, I'm sorry," the doctor said. "You should have sent someone to get me. I would have come."

She got up from the bench and wrung her plump hands and began to pace up and down. Father, oh Father, she said to herself, you should have let me come with you for once. What am I to do without you? She searched quickly through one pocket and then another until she found a peppermint. She popped the candy into her mouth and rolled it about her tender gums. She felt the relief of its sweetness meeting her stomach. Then she felt the doctor's warm hands, leading her back to the bench.

Her breasts jiggled as she sat down. What could she do? A man always did that. They always left women with the consequences. He made the decisions, she was left with the mess. And all because of Eve.

The doctor sat down beside her and stroked her arm. "I would have come," he said once again.

She shrugged free of his touch. "And what difference would it make to call you? You couldn't have stopped him. He wanted to go and so he went."

"I suppose you're right," the doctor said.

"And to think of it, one dozen two-quart sealers dills," she said. "And I couldn't even give him one."

She watched as far above her the fireball wavered and began to loose its shape. Then the top of it sank to meet the bottom and the sides of it spilled out into the morning sky.

The Wild Plum Tree

Mr. Malcolm,
English 100

Betty Lafreniere

ESSAY

The Wild Plum Tree

It is more than a shrub but not a tree, bark is smooth
when young. Inside, white sapwood, porous bark splits with
age and leaves
narrow tipped, fruit slightly reddish with blood
flowers showy white gracing
southern end of Manitoba and other provinces,
of no commercial value.

Mr. Malcolm is English 100. He is also Betty's mathematics teacher, history teacher and language arts teacher. He is straight from Jamaica and looks to pregnant wayward girls and delinquents to teach him all they know about Manitoba.

"Now surely," he says, "you must know more about this subject. It was your free choice."

Betty shrugs, feigns indifference. The essay is the best she can do under the circumstances. The reference books in the classroom are *The Book of Knowledge* and *Weeds, Trees and Wildflowers in Canada*. Some of the girls have taken a bus down to the public library on William Avenue. But not her. What she doesn't know, she will make up. That's life, she tells herself.

"But you see, I asked for six pages, at least," he says. He wears pastel colours. Pale green polyester pants, a pinkish tie against a coral-coloured shirt. She ignores him, looks out the dusty window down into the city. The rapid darting of traffic intrigues her. Where are all these people going to, coming from? And why? It seems pointless. She saw shadows in the graveyard last night. She'd sat on the radiator in her room looking out and thought, how appropriate: a graveyard in the back yard of the home for wayward girls. They were all burying things, their past, their present, the things that came out of them. And she saw shadows down there, lithe phantoms sprinting from tree to tree, leaping up from the hard granite stones. Today, several of the tombstones are toppled into the grass. The praying virgin with her blind eyes and reverent posture, hands held up in frozen supplication, lies on one side.

"Did you not understand my instructions then?" the teacher asks.

"Yes, Mr. Malcolm, I understood your instructions." She wants only to be left alone.

"Mr. Jackson."

"Yes, Mr. Jackson." His name is Malcolm P. Jackson. You have never heard the sound of a mob, he has told them. He'd sat on the desk in front of them, swinging his knees in and out, like a young child needing to urinate. I was a boy when I once heard such a mob. It was like the sound of a swarm of angry bees growing louder and louder. Let me tell you, it was not a pleasant sound. Angry people. A mob rushing along the street. I was very young but I learned quickly to be afraid of the mob.

"Well then, if you knew the instructions, why have you handed me this?" He holds up the single sheet of paper. The classroom has grown quiet. The girls stop talking to listen.

"Because I felt like it."

Several of the girls titter. Betty has not said this for their benefit. She only needs, wants, to be left on her own. A detention is a way to accomplish this end. Mr. Jackson sets the paper down, takes a piece of yellow chalk from his shirt pocket and rolls it from hand to hand.

"My dear girl. Listen. In my country, education is a privilege. Only the cleverest people go beyond grade school. Our parents made great sacrifices for us. We're grateful. With us, it is never a question, whether we feel like it or not; we do it."

"If you're so smart," someone says, "then why are you here with us?"

He pretends he hasn't heard, but the muscles in his jaw contract suddenly as though he just bit into a stone.

Betty wants no part of their taunting. She wants to be away from them all, to be able to sift through all the information she has gathered, to make some order of it.

"Surely you could do better than this," he persists. "There must be more you could write about the wild plum tree."

Even now, she smells the fruit of it. The tart flavour, taut skin splitting in her mouth, the slippery membrane of its meat, a piece of slime at the bottom of a quart sealer jar of home-made wine coming suddenly into her mouth like a great clot of blood. There is too much to say about the wild plum tree. The assignment has paralyzed her.

"Yes, Chocolate Drop. I'm sure there is." She uses the girls' private name for Mr. Jackson.

His nostrils flare. The room grows silent. Then laughter erupts, spills over. "Chocolate Drop," a girl says and then they all say, "Chocolate Drop."

His eyes dart about the room. Betty continues to stand before the window, toying with the frayed cord on the venetian blind. Thousands of girls have stood at this very same window and played with this cord. It's marked with their anguish, their boredom and frustrations.

"Well um," Mr. Jacksons says, bouncing the chalk from palm to palm. "Well um." The palms of his hands are tinged pink. The skin has been worn away. It's from masturbating, flogging his meat, the girls say. He clutches at his crotch frequently in the classroom. Adjusts his testicles before he sits down on the edge of the desk to confront them.

"Who needs you, Chocolate Drop?" a girl asks.

"Well, Miss," Mr. Jackson says to Betty, "you see what you have instigated? You may call me what you like. What can one expect from Satan's daughter?"

Betty yanks the frayed cord. It snaps free and falls to the floor. Several of the girls leave their desks. Mr. Jackson turns and faces them quickly. "Well um," he says. "That will be ten pages now. You seem to think she is a humorous person. Do you think ten pages is also funny?"

They groan. "You can't make us do ten pages," a tall girl with angry grey eyes says.

He strides to his desk, pulls open a drawer and takes out a wooden ruler. "Ten pages, I said." He bangs the ruler against his desk.

"Fuck off," the tall girl says.

He walks swiftly to her and whacks her across the face with the ruler. Smiles fade, all movement is suspended. A red welt rises on the girl's cheek. "And who else wishes to express themselves in such a manner?" he asks. The girls one by one return to their desks.

"You heard her," Betty says. "Go fuck yourself in Jamaica and leave us alone." A flood of tension is released suddenly. She feels the teacher's wooden ruler bounce off her shoulder blade. The girls laugh and call out their individual hate names for Mr. Jackson. An eraser bounces off the wall beside his head. He backs slowly over to the classroom door and stands with one hand on the knob. His lips are flecked with spittle. "Ten pages, you naughty spoiled children. When you can control yourselves, we will continue this class," he says and flees.

Control yourselves. Is it lack of control then, that has brought them all to this place? The windowpane is cool against Betty's forehead as she looks down into the street. A young man cuts through the cemetery, hands plunged deep into his pockets; he walks with his shoulders hunched up, a cigarette hangs from his mouth. He glances up at the window where she stands and is gone.

Notes for essay on wild plum tree
Mr. Malcolm, English 100

the beginning

Suddenly you face across the street where once there was only a coulee with bullrushes, twitch grass four feet high, God and Indian arrowheads, a brand new house.

But first, machines squashed frogs and garter snakes and a pen once lost and never found and then ploughed them beneath tons of landfill from a field where they also discovered the skeletons part of which Laurence brought to school. (the skull)

Then, when the four-and-a-half member family move into that new house, the dark-haired woman has a bump in front so she

is probably pregnant (being the oldest of six teaches you to
watch for those things); the beginning ends.

through yellowing lace curtains
I have always watched
the games of others
hiding and seeking the waning sun
shadows the mourning dove's
spotted grey
bird sounds temper the shrill play
sounds
that strike my note
of sorrow
I have not found anything good
in tomorrow

notes   before the beginning

Leaves (somewhat hairy) of the dog mustard plant, which,
like the mother of seven, originated in Europe and was first
found in Canada at Emerson in 1922, tickle bare legs when
walking in the coulee. And their flower, clusters of pale yellow
stain white organdy, which also scratches bare legs when
walking, sitting, standing, period. When you wander with
Laurence in the coulee, he carries your shoes and you can
feel the spongy ground and make it squeeze up between your
toes and then he shows you his hidden pool

and in the deep pool
melted snow yellows
bright all the dead grasses
pink granite stones and your face
rising and falling as feet dipped clean
drip the surface and make you wrinkle

Russian pigweed stands as high as you because you are eight,
but Laurence's head is a little above it. The plant is like the

two of you, one plant and two different kinds of flowers, male and female.

And God is also in the coulee, moving before you. You can feel His breath on your body, coming through the organdy you have worn especially for Him because it is Sunday.

And Laurence, even though he does not go to any church, is of the same plant that nods in the same breath. But for some reason, the mother of seven doesn't think so which is why you walk among the Russian pigweed, so she can't see you and get angry and send you down the road to your grandfather's house to get a lesson in the Bible.

God you were
there inside
my knees and elbows
scratched raw
crawling from imaginary
Indians
would take my yellow hair
make a belt or something, God
your voice
fades faster than games
of Indians don't last
forever

"Betty uses foul language and shows disrespect for the property of the institution," the social worker says. She reads from the teacher's report. She wears black cat's-eyes-shaped glasses and adjusts them before she speaks again. Betty can feel her father's shyness of this woman, his eagerness to appease and have everyone agree quickly that everything will be fine so that he can go home and report to Mika with a clear conscience that he's done his best. He sits on a chair beside Betty. They face the social worker's desk beneath the window. The room is a basement room. The window is at street level and Betty watches and counts the feet of people who pass by on the sidewalk.

"If you won't adhere to the rules of this institution, what choice will we have, but to ask you to leave it?"

"Certainly, she's going to follow the rules and regulations," Maurice says. "There's no maybe about it."

He plays with the brim of his hat and looks down at the floor. He's put on his suit and tie and taken the bus in from the country especially for this meeting. He's deeply embarrassed. He cannot bring himself to say the words, "pregnant" and "social worker."

The woman writes something on her pad. Betty wonders if she is writing, "Father is co-operative," or "Supportive father." With whom and of whom?

"What about rules regarding hitting students with rulers?" Betty asks.

"Listen here," Maurice says, suddenly irritated. "What makes you think you can ask that, eh? You're not in any position here to ask questions."

"And what position am I in?"

Maurice is flustered. He twirls the hat between his thick brown fingers, clears his throat several times.

The social worker gets up quickly. "I think the two of you need to talk alone. It's important that we reach an understanding today." The door closes behind her. Maurice relaxes. He wipes his brow, sits up straighter and looks about the room for the first time. The walls are cement block, unpainted. There are no pictures. "This here place is not so bad," he says. "I don't know what you're griping about."

A black mongrel zig-zags across the boulevard and sidewalk. It stops and looks down into the room, sniffs and then continues on its way.

"You don't have to live here. I hate it."

"Well now, that wasn't our doing, was it?" Maurice says. It's the closest he's come to mentioning her pregnancy. "Anyway, it's a darn sight better than being out on the street because, believe you me, that's where you're headed if you don't shape up."

Betty stifles the urge to laugh. Shape up. She is rapidly shaping up. She knows that her parents' number one concern is her shape. They're afraid that she might be expelled from the home and shame them with her bulging presence in the community. It's the only reason for his trip into the city. She knows she's been cut off, that she can't look to either of her parents for anything.

"It's okay," she says. "I'll be okay now. It's just been hard to adjust."

Maurice brightens. He looks at her with a wide smile, his eyes uneasy though, carefully avoiding looking at her stomach. "Adjust, absolutely. I can understand that. Certainly it takes time to get used to new situations."

"Losing your home is a new situation all right."

"Eh?" His hands stop in mid-air.

"I feel as though I have no home." For one second she wants to fling herself at him, bury her face into his shoulder and hold on.

Maurice works furiously as he flicks nonexistent lint from his hat.

"Well, that's not quite so," he says. "You've still got a home. You're only here for a few more months, that's all. Once it's over, it's over." He stands up and puts his hat on, adjusts the brim. "You've learned."

I am learning to control myself, no more fucking. "In a few more months, I'll have my baby." She wants him to think about this.

"On that score your mother and I agree. You can't bring the bastard home." He takes his wallet from his pocket. "Just in case you need something," he says and hands her several bills. His hands are shaking. She takes the money from him. Everything is okay, taken care of, he'll tell Mika. You know, it's not easy, it takes time to adjust to these things. All she needed was a little talk and a little time. He's in a hurry, anxious to be away.

"I have to go," she says.

The door closes behind him. She waits. She sees his feet pass by on the sidewalk along with the feet of another person, strangers passing by.

notes for the essay   Bible lessons at Opah's

Opah means Grandfather. Omah means Grandmother. (This is for the benefit of Mr. Malcolm, English 100, the Chocolate Drop who came directly from Jamaica and wants to know everything he can about Canada.)

The lesson for today, Opah says, is: HOW GOD LED HIS PEOPLE OUT OF THE LAND OF EGYPT. But then he forgets and his sky-blue eyes melt into the horizon and he speaks of hundreds of people gathering around twenty-eight train cars in Russia. They are coming, these people, like the dog mustard, only a year later, to spread out across the fields of southern Manitoba. Faith is the Victory, Faith is the Victory, Opah hums, wiping tears from his face and Omah comes out from the pantry wiping hands of flour onto her apron. There is a boy in the garden, she says. When she goes to call him in, he runs away, she explains, worried. They still dream of thieves and Bolshevik murderers. Laurence is waiting for the lesson to be finished so that there will be someone to go fishing with. He has only one friend because he is on welfare.

First you learn, Opah says, no longer can you get into heaven free because of your parents or grandparents. When you're twelve, you're on your own with God.

He makes you learn the ten commandments even though you know Emily, who lives across the road, whose father is a doctor and drives a Lincoln and with his money has built the gingerbread house that now has a patio and one more

child added, which looks out over another row of houses
where the coulee once was, this girl, whose father's building
also destroyed an Indian burial ground, will not hesitate to
walk across the friendship and go fishing with Laurence.

– round-leaved mallow is different from common mallow and
is a nuisance only in the prairie provinces where it nudges
aside Kentucky Blue and Shady Nook grass but that doesn't
matter because you can't really eat cultured lawn the way you
can the nutlets of round mallow an after school treat
not double bubble gum or fudgsicles but a prairie weed that
stayed behind to live in town to colour green your teeth you
forgot to brush today but ants don't brush do they or for that
matter neither do grasshoppers they squirt tobacco –

too bad   Emily can't eat round-leaved mallow
too bad   she has to eat juicy fruit cracker jack and all that crap
too bad   she isn't a grasshopper or an ant

I would press her lightly with my toe and scare the shit out
of her.

Emily is a stinking willie.
She is poisonous inside.
To her, fishing with Laurence is an opportunity to practise
lying. She is like a plum rotting in the grass.

I lost Laurence one summer
didn't last and he was gone
I looked: in the garden
            in the poolroom
            bowling alley
            cafe
            fair grounds
no Laurence

Look – he has waited long enough for you to go fishing.
It's your fault you learned the ten commandments.

And now, Emily wears his arrowhead around her neck. Your
arrowheads gather dust in a cigarette box in the rafters of the

icehouse while she, whose backyard has a patio surrounded by stinking willie, wears his arrowhead because plum wine is strong enough inside Laurence that no longer does he care that occasionally he is on welfare or that at ten he had lice.

The small lamp in the corner on the table spreads a pink glow in the room. There are six girls in various stages of pregnancy dressed in bathrobes, feet tucked up beneath them, one lies flat on her back, she is only in her third month. "When I get out of this place I'm going to slash the bugger's tires, all four of them," the girl with the angry grey eyes says. They have been telling 'how I lost my virginity' stories. Betty listens, she has not contributed and she knows they expect her to soon. She thinks that only this tall girl has been honest.

"I used to tell my parents I was staying at a friend's house," one of the girls says. "They never checked, usually they never checked, that is. Then one time, wouldn't you know it, my girlfriend's father answered the phone before she could get to it? And made her tell my Dad where I was? God, I almost died. There I was, Rick was doing it to me, you get what I mean? He didn't even knock—"

"Doing what?"

"Aw, come on, you know—"

"Was it big, small, did it hurt? You've got to tell a better story than that."

"I opened my eyes and saw my father. He just stood there staring and didn't say anything. It gave me the creeps. Like, for a minute, I didn't know what he was going to do. Then he went and waited for me in the car. When I came out he was sitting there crying. I felt like a piece of shit."

The girls moan sympathetically. They stare at their feet, at the space in front of them. They are all getting into shape, out of control, Betty thinks. Sometimes one of their boyfriends visits and then the rest of them slouch in corners, snapping gum, dissatisfied until he leaves. Where's your boyfriend, they've asked Betty, sixty-five girls who have eaten too many sweets, superior because they have visitors, more righteous for a time, than her.

They turn to her. They wait now for her story to begin. I was fourteen. He was an old man. At first he just used his finger. I screwed sixteen men this year and have written their names down in a scribbler.

"His name is Frank," she says. "We're in love. He wants to marry me."

The tall grey-eyed girl rises first and the others follow her one by one and file out of the lounge. Woolworth diamonds sparkle on their fingers. Now, at last, she can be alone.

notes for the essay   hiding and seeking

Laurence's anger moves in circles, his teeth on edge against an unnamed foe burned off in the sound of his motorcycle held into place by centrifugal force around and around. His anger spent, the dust settling, he stops moving, stands beside you and finally you are once again behind him, your arms about his narrow leather waist climbing the yellow fields, cutting a swathe through black-headed cattails (fire torches, good for eating) in the ditches beside the highway, up and down Main Street. He doesn't speak, but only with others does he need to, you never cared, his silence was like a lady slipper growing beside a swampy marsh. He takes the old skull from his saddle bag, lines it up on Main Street, takes a run at it and shatters the old bone like pieces of coconut shell skittering curses across a table top. Don't do it, you think, but it's his skull, he can do what he wants. You ride and drink until the sun is down behind old weathered caved-in barns and he pukes plum wine, purple and violent in the grass at your feet. He lies you down and you are surprised at his fumbling, thought he would know how to do it better and so you help him with his clothing and guide him. (Was it big, was it fat or small, did it hurt? Come on, you've got to tell a better story than that.)

His nostril in your eye and when he turns his head you notice: hair in his ear, dirty. Emily, Emily, he says, not your name, but hers and his nostrils puff out warm plum air and his mouth, not gentle, smells of sour jam as he pins you to the earth but the worst is that after, he pulls grass from your hair, says he's sorry and treats you like a friend.

you are –

Listening until the sound of the engine is a distant whine on the highway, an angry wasp, a wavering line of sound straightening, becoming threadlike, thin, and then it snaps and –

Betty switches off the lamp. The traffic below in the city street is a ribbon connecting people together. The gravestones sheltered beneath the trees seem to move in the light filtering down between the tree branches. She hears a sharp whistle like a signal, and the figures rise up from among the stones, gather beneath the streetlight and plan their night errands. She watches and waits for tomorrow.

The Day My
Grandfather Died

I REMEMBER the day I bought a small bottle of Evening in Paris cologne. I was on my way home from school at lunch time and took the long way home, going down Main Street and past the drugstore instead of cutting through the coulee as I usually did, because I wanted to see the display of cologne in the window. My friend Claudette Gagnon had seen it earlier and told me about it. Claudette wore a cardigan sweater that had poodles and pom poms on it and a black 'Frederick's of Hollywood' type brassiere beneath her sweater which gathered her breasts up into swollen jiggling shelves of jelly. She also shaved off her eyebrows and painted them back on in a thin coquettish black arch. Wherever I went with her a residue of attention, like dandruff, fell on me. But for me, the attraction of Claudette was more than that. Claudette was French, as was my father. I had even picked up her accent and went out of my way to say things such as, "The car, she is parked in the drive-way," and, "H'it's going to rain."

"For Pete's sake," Mika, my mother, would say, "your English is worse than mine. You sound as bad as the Lafrenieres." Which made me smile because to be like the Lafrenieres, my father's people, would make my rebellion complete and finally take me out and away from the rest of the family.

"From Bourjois of Paris and Montreal," the display card in the drugstore read. Blue bottles the shape of uteruses nestled down inside the blue satin-lined boxes. I unscrewed the cap from the sample bottle. The smell of cologne was like almonds. It made me ache in "that place" and I would have liked to have touched and gentled myself until the bud flowered. But the warning I'd received from Mika was profound and clear. "Play with yourself and you'll never want a man," she said. And I knew that I wanted a man, eventually. At that time, I was still like a dog chasing a car, barking and nipping at boys' heels, not knowing what I'd do if I ever caught one.

I stood there in the drugstore, getting off, as they say, on the smell of Evening in Paris cologne. It reminded me of a mystery novel I'd once read. It was a story about a short bald man who murdered beautiful but cruel women who laughed at him. The women were either blonde and cold or brunette and very shallow. They all had long hair and wore skin-tight black sheath dresses and rhinestone jewelry. They smoked cigarettes using a holder. I liked the bald man. He had impeccable manners and manicured fingernails. I thought that killing people for laughing at you was justifiable homicide. According to the novel, he would smile a sinister smile as he took a silver box from his pocket and flicked open the lid. The woman continued to laugh heartlessly through a curl of cigarette smoke while he offered her a deadly candied almond. Then it was his turn to laugh as death came slowly and the victim's contorted features made her ugly in the end.

The smell of the cologne reminded me of my mother walking to the corner to catch the Greyhound into Winnipeg. She carried a shopping bag on her arm. She wore her navy suit which displayed her trim figure, a pink frilly blouse and a navy pillbox hat. I carried a box for her, filled with mittens and scarves which her women's church group had made. All winter they'd met weekly in each others' homes. I despised their fervent good works and their complete lack of adornment. It made them seem unnatural and grimly severe. They seldom smiled. My mother had been elected to take the results of their labours into the city and deliver them to a mission. I swung the box up into the baggage department.

"She's one 'eavy box," I complained. My mother stared at me and then laughed. Her laughter was seldom an expression of joy or good humour. Her laughter said things such as: see, I knew that would happen, or, trust me, the world's a dirty place.

One time, her laughter was spontaneous. I was walking across the yard towards the house and she was standing, framed by the window, looking out at me. For a terrible second I had the feeling that I was looking into a mirror and seeing my own reflection in her face and so I didn't watch where I was going. I stepped on a rake that had been left lying and it sprung up and bonked me between the eyes. My mother began to laugh outright, a deep belly laugh. When I came into the house she was still laughing. And I learned that the way to make her happy was to hurt yourself.

The bus driver swung the baggage door closed. Mika hid the remainder of her laughter behind a pink glove. Just as I was turning away, stinging and angry, she touched my arm. "What would you like me to bring you from the city?"

And I said, "Candied almonds."

When she came home that night, she had them with her and when I opened up the bag, the sight of those lilac, pink, yellow and white candies affected me strangely. I sat cross-legged on the couch with the bag in my lap and played with the seed-shaped candies. The texture of them was like that of a very fine toadstool, pebbly and cool to the touch. They made my heart ache. In the same way my mother pinched her babies to express affection, in the same way my berserk hormones made me want to laugh and cry simultaneously or dream beneath musk-scented sheets of caressing and being caressed, and then recoiling in anger and hitting out when someone tried to touch me—I wanted to crush the candied almonds underfoot. I couldn't help but think about the images that the mystery novel had evoked, and about the possibility of some demented grey person in Eaton's candy department slipping a few poisoned almonds into the candy bin. And so I shared my gift, offered the candies up to my mother and to my sisters instead of eating them myself. While they sucked, I watched for the signs, the deep pain in the stomach, the sudden clutching and pitching forward, their expressions when they became aware of their own finality.

The smell of the cologne in the drugstore that day was like that act. It was power, it was anger and knowing something that no one else knew. And so I bought a bottle.

I took my purchase to the clerk. She rang it up on the cash register and slipped the cologne into a bag. Then she looked at me as though she'd only just seen me. "Have you been home for lunch yet?" she asked. She searched my face with a prying, knowing look. She was over forty years old and so I'd never bothered to remember her name. I knew her only by her breasts. They were enormous. The boys called her Tits Wiggle. I handed her the money. "No, I haven't, why?" What's it to you? Drop off, eh? Flake off, peel off, bug off, take a flying leap.

"It's not for me to say," the clerk said. "You'd just better get going. Go straight home."

I left the drugstore slowly, so as not to let her know that I was concerned. But as soon as I was clear of the window and her sight, I began to run. I knew something terrible must have happened if she wouldn't say what it was. And when I got home, I found out my Grandfather Thiessen had died.

"Guess what," I said to Claudette. "My grandfather kicked the bucket during the night."

"Yeah, so I heard. That's tough."

"He was eighty-one years old; it was no surprise."

We'd met at the Scratching Chicken Hotel cafe during the noon break. My mother was away, sitting with my grandmother. Claudette didn't take her lunch to school as most of the farm kids did. Claudette wasn't farm. She'd been expelled from the convent school at Grande Pointe where she lived with her parents who owned Gagnon Chevy-Olds garage. I'd never been to Grande Pointe, but the kids said if you didn't speak French, no one would talk to you. I always ate my own lunch at home and then rode my bike downtown so that I could sit with Claudette while she ate hers. She was talkative, flashy and demonstrative, traits that I then attributed to her French-Canadian identity only because I didn't see these traits in my mother or my grandparents, who were not French, but Mennonite, a fact that I detested. Being Mennonite was like having acne. It was shameful, dreary. No one invited you out. How to be French, I didn't know. My father was seldom home and when he was, showed no interest or energy, I didn't know which, in perpetuating any of his own traditions.

"I had a cat once," Claudette said. "She was my cat for twelve years. Slept on my bed every night. When she passed off, I really felt bad. I 'ad her since I was a kid." She nudged me with her elbow. "You'll be okay. H'it takes time."

We'd all buried animals. I remembered my dog, Laddie, a collie stray. My grandfather had persuaded my mother to let me keep him. He used to take my hand in his mouth and walk me to school. Claudette's sympathetic nudge unsettled me. I squashed a drinking straw flat, rolled it into a ball and flicked it across the counter into the chocolate bars. "I had my grandfather since I was a kid too," I said.

"I guess, eh?" Claudette said and snickered. "I like you, you're bad." She pushed her plate of chips aside and ran her fingers through her thick black hair which she wore short and which met at the back of her head like a feathered duck's tail. She had tiny features and large eyes. We sat side by side with our arms resting on the counter. I was tanned deeply, a dusty dark brown, and she was very fair. I was the only Lafreniere to have black hair and I felt special, set apart. Today, people mistake me for Jewish or Italian.

"I guess he died of old age, eh?"

"Cancer. I think. I kind of lost touch."

"Jeez. Tough. I guess you'll miss him."

I didn't feel one thing or another. My face was a little numb as though I'd just been to the dentist, that was all. I shrugged. "He was sick for a long time. The only thing I really remember about him was that he ate a lot of sunflower seeds. Every pocket, full of seeds, and he'd spit the shells out through his mustache into his hand. His hands were always moist. I didn't like it."

"No kidding." Claudette had grown tired of the topic. She played with the silver cross at her neck and her features had a painful bored expression. Coffee gurgled down from the tops of the coffee makers into the glass urns below. The waitress came over and began to clean up the dishes.

"Let's cut," Claudette said. "This place stinks."

We walked down Main Street, passed by the corner where we should have turned to go to school. "What's up?" I asked, surprised.

"On the day your grandfather died, you shouldn't have to go to school," Claudette said. "My parents, they went into the city for parts today. We can have the place for ourselves."

We cut school that afternoon. We walked, instead, to the outskirts of Agassiz and stuck out our thumbs. Two rides and we were at Grande Pointe. The town was a disappointment. I was looking forward to something more than the jumbled collection of buildings and houses on either side of the wide dirt street that cut away from the main highway and rejoined it a mile later. I wanted more than street signs written in French. Gagnon Chevy-Olds was the newest-looking building on the street. As we drew near, I saw an old man sitting on a painted chair.

"Who's that?"

"It's just my father's uncle," Claudette said. "My father lets him hang around the garage. He's got nothing better to do. Don't worry, he won't say anything about us being here. Half the time he doesn't know what day it is."

He wore a straw hat and grey wool pants and a white shirt, unbuttoned at the neck. The kind my father wore around the house. He beckoned to Claudette and began speaking to her softly, haltingly, in French. His wide face was calm, gentle, no will to harm in it. If someone said to him, tomorrow the world will end, he would reply, so be it.

Claudette leaned over him. "Speak English," she said loudly. "Can't you see I've got company? This is Lureen Lafreniere. She's a girl from school."

He looked at me, took off his straw hat and rested it on his knee. My mouth tingled. If I smiled, my face would be forever frozen in that position. I thought I'd recognized that gesture, the wide sweeping of his hand. He spoke again, and to me his voice was like the sound of newspapers being swept along the street by the wind.

"He thinks he knows your old man," Claudette said.

"Oh yeah?" My heart lifted.

"Wants to know if you're Prosper's daughter," she laughed. "Prosper Lafreniere was an old hermit, older than him. He died last year. I told you, the old guy's cuckoo." She made a winding motion at her temple.

"Tell him that my father's the barber at Agassiz. His name is Maurice. He used to play the fiddle."

She told him. I held my breath. I needed to know something of who I hoped I was.

"I don't remember your father. Was he of this place?"

"Told you, screws loose. Come on, forget it," Claudette said and began to walk away.

The old man lifted his hat, waved it at me. "Adios to youse girls," he said and laughed. I liked him and wished that Claudette hadn't spoken to him with so little respect.

I followed Claudette between two buildings to the back of the garage. There were sounds of hammering coming from the garage. Through windows in a door, I could see bright splashes of sparks from a welder. Claudette stood on her toes so that she could see inside. "Good," she said. "Jimmy's working today."

"Who?"

"Jimmy Nabess. He works on and off for my father. He's cute." She winked. "Maybe later, I'll invite him to come up."

We went up a flight of stairs. She unlocked the door, stepped inside. A gold crucifix hung above the door. She led me through a small kitchen into the living room. A trestle table rested along one wall; along another, pine bookshelves with knick-knacks on them, a highback wooden bench, and beside the bench a pine couch with burlap cushions. A spinning wheel sat in the corner by the window. Above the couch, there were dark paintings of a fort and Indians huddled around a fire, tepees in the background. Another painting: a cobblestone street leading to an old church and tall European-looking buildings with narrow windows, lining the street.

"Nice," I said.

"You think so? I don't. I think it's crap. My mother had a vacation in Quebec and came back with it. It's like living in a coffin," she said. "Be back in a sec." She went into the kitchen. A moment later she stuck her head around the corner. "Do you like your beer warm or cold? I keep a case under my bed if you want a warm one."

I took her love for beer as being part of her French identity and so I said I'd love a warm beer. I went over to the front window and looked out over the town. There was more to Grande Pointe than I'd first seen. I could see the peaks of houses across the river, where the town unfolded in neat rows among lime-green groves of maple trees. It looked like Agassiz, no different. The same muddy river that divided Grande Pointe ran along the edge of Agassiz as well and the same flotsam on that river, the bloated bodies of cows, broken trees, tin cans, passed through their town as it did ours. Claudette came back with the beer.

I watched as she tipped the bottle, there was a gurgling, and one quarter of the beer was gone. "They put beer in babies' bottles, the French," my mother said once, referring to my father's relatives. "So that they can go out to dances, they take the kids with them, fill their bottles with beer so the kids will fall asleep in the car, and they can have all the fun they want."

"And so, what's wrong with that?" Maurice said.

And she said, "If they could only see, realize, the damage they're doing to their children."

I tipped my bottle, parted my lips the way Claudette had, but the beer didn't flow down my throat. It foamed, backed up into my nose, stinging. My eyes watered. Claudette laughed and brought me a Kleenex. I asked for a glass and drank the first beer and talked about the other kids at school, some of the boys in our class; and I was surprised that the boys I had gone through elementary school with and now high school, and who

I thought were disgusting, she thought attractive. I liked the homestead old feeling of her rough, wooden living room and she wanted a modern one like mine. A feeling of disillusionment was setting in along with a slight light-headedness. Claudette yawned, looked at her watch. "Be back in a sec," she said once again. "I'm going to talk to Jimmy. Help yourself to another beer."

I went into Claudette's bedroom. There were clothes scattered about on the bed and cosmetics over the top of her dresser. I looked into the mirror. "Goodness, who is she?" Mika had said once when I was changing, my features rearranging themselves weekly during puberty, giving me at last a broad face, a too-thick nose and deepset eyes, too small; I tried to do tricks with cosmetics but it didn't help.

"She doesn't even look like a Lafreniere," Mika said and it was true. Several times I'd seen my father's brothers, and they were both short and fat and small-featured. I pulled my hair up and away, held it into a pony tail, tight, so that my eyes became slanted. Sometimes I thought I was Oriental, or Eskimo. I saw Claudette's blue bottle of Evening in Paris cologne. I dabbed some behind my ears and then took another beer out from under her bed.

"And this," Claudette said, entering the bedroom suddenly, "is my friend Lureen, the one I told you about?" She introduced me to Jimmy Nabess. Jimmy was Indian. He was short and slender; his hair, almost shoulder-length, was caught back behind his ears. He wore a baseball cap, a satin-looking blue jacket with his name on one shoulder, and dusty blue jeans.

"Hi ya," he said. His expression said that he didn't care if I lived or died.

"I told him we're having a party, and he wanted to come too. Hurry up and finish that beer. Parties are more fun if you're drunk."

For the next hour, we drank beer steadily, almost duti-
fully, as Claudette worked hard to fill each awkward silence,
the trailing off of conversation. Jimmy and I sat side by side on
the couch. I grew quieter and quieter because I sensed his
dislike for me. Finally, despairing, Claudette said that what
we needed was some music and went to her bedroom to get
her records. Jimmy moved forward on the couch as though
he were about to follow her and then changed his mind, took
off his jacket and began squeezing bottle caps. I noted that our
arms were almost the same colour.

"You from Grande Pointe?" I asked.

"Uhuh."

I didn't know if this meant yes or no. "It seems like an
okay place."

"It's the same like any place."

"Nabess," I said. "Is that French?"

"No."

I didn't want to ask him what it was. "Lafreniere is French.
My father speaks French."

He shrugged impatiently. "So what's the big deal? Lots
of people talk French. Claudette," he called. "I'm dry."

"Coming, coming," Claudette said and put a record on
the player. She clapped her hands and began to do the twist.
The beer had made her face flushed, her eyes shine. "Hey
come on," she said. "Let's dance."

"I hafta get back to work. Your old man will be the first
one to kick my ass if I don't."

"Just one," she said.

They danced for a full hour. I watched for awhile. They
were caught up in their dancing, in each other. Occasionally
Claudette would suggest that he ask me to dance, but only
half-heartedly, and when she turned the record over, she went
back to him. I got up from the couch. The room tilted. I walked
over to the window. I saw the old man, he was crossing the

street slowly. He walked, choosing each step as though it were his last. He stood in front of the cafe, shielded his eyes and looked in the window, searching for someone. Then he began walking down the street to the corner.

I willed his faltering steps, each rising and falling of his feet. He belonged in the picture above the couch, an old man walking along a cobblestone street. It seemed to me that he was no ordinary person, but larger. I wanted to walk beside him with my arm under his and claim him as my ancestor. I leaned with my forehead against the glass and the cool window-pane felt good against my stiff face. My breath was reflected back to me. I smelled sour beer and something else, the Evening in Paris cologne.

The smell of the cologne reminded me of fruit cake, almond paste and my grandparents standing with a tray loaded with chunks of dark fruit cake at their fiftieth wedding anniversary. Grandma wore a loose-fitting white dress made of some light material that did not show her large body, but hid it so instead of looking fat and awkward, she seemed to float. She wore gold leaves in her white hair and so as they approached me, I thought she was a vision, a fairy godmother who had the power to grant wishes. And I would have asked her to take away my aches and pains. I was never without sore limbs, "growing pains," my mother called them, and an uneasy stomach. I did not think they were growing pains. I felt that my bones were going to crack and splinter because of some inner pressure. I would have asked my grandmother to make me feel happiness. But she frowned at the tray of cake my grandfather carried and said, "Nah, Papa, look at what you've done. You've cut far too much cake. It will only be wasted." And the fairy vision vanished.

"Give it to the children, then," he said. And it came to me how their conversations always seemed to centre on food, the growing of it, the preparing of it and the eating. That was all that mattered. To me, their lives had been narrow and confining; even here, now, at a celebration, they were unable to step across the limits and celebrate. I was angry and so I said, "Don't waste the food on us kids, feed it to the bloody pigs instead."

The old man had reached the corner. He seemed to hesitate and then he turned sharply to the left and began crossing a bridge which spanned the same river that flowed past my grandparents' cottage. I could see that river through the leaves of the vine arbour where I was sent as punishment, to reflect in solitude upon what I'd said about feeding good food to the pigs. Two words my grandfather forbade us to use because he said we didn't know their meanings: starve and hate. I knew my words had cut him deeply. There were several boys playing along the river bank trying to skip stones and I forgot about what it was I should be thinking as I watched and wished I were down there to show them how to do it and at the same time, make them feel stupid. Grandfather came in and sat down beside me. He didn't speak for a long time and then asked, "Why are you always so angry?"

"I guess I was born that way. I can't help it. I couldn't help being born."

"Not so, not so," he said. "God made a much brighter girl."

His way of speaking irritated me. "If you say so, then it must be true."

He pulled at my chin in an attempt to have me look at him. His hand smelled of sunflower seeds. His pale blue eyes were moist with sorrow. I couldn't explain my anger. I thought I was a freak, I didn't belong because I was totally different from every other member of that family.

"People make me mad," I said.

"I'm sorry for you, then. Because you become their slave when you let them make you angry. Being angry doesn't change anything. You can never change what people say and do. The only thing you can change in this world is your reaction to what they say and do. You're hurting yourself by being angry. Look here," he said. He took his penknife from his pocket. He cut a **v** into a vine leaf, lightly, barely perceptible. "When you come for German lessons on Saturday, I'll show you what anger does."

The following Saturday, the scar in the leaf had become deep and brown and the leaf had grown, but was misshapen. "That's what you're doing with your life," he said. "With your anger you make marks in it that will never go away."

He left me to think on this. I thought. I thought he was minimizing what I was feeling with cheap tricks with a penknife. I went into the garden. I picked up the hoe. I chopped and hacked until I had cut down all of his sunflowers.

I turned from the window, feeling morose and angry at the same time for Claudette's lack of attention to me. And for the first time I wondered, how was I going to get home?

"My mother will kill me," I said. "I think I'd better head for home."

Claudette danced over to me, stuck her fingers into my chest and pushed me backwards towards the couch without missing a beat of the music. "You can't go yet. Jimmy wants to have a dance with you."

She brought me another beer and put on a record. It was a slow song. She put her arms around Jimmy's neck, he put his hands around her waist and his leg between hers and they moved in time to the music.

I belched loudly. My stomach was swollen and felt full. I was in a haze, stupified, and so I lay down. Through half-closed eyes, I saw Jimmy place his hand on Claudette's breast, his hand, brown, against her pale blue sweater and I thought, he shouldn't do that, he's squashing the pom poms on her poodles. "Oh no," Claudette said in response to something Jimmy had whispered in her ear, "not with her here."

My stomach heaved and the room swung violently. I had heard that if you're drunk and the room moves, lie with one foot resting on the floor and the motion will stop. I tried that and closed my eyes. It didn't work. I smelled something thickly sweet, it was the Evening in Paris cologne and it made my stomach even queasier. Claudette laughed drunkenly. Jimmy manoeuvred her across the floor towards the bedroom door with his pelvis. He backed her up against the wall and kissed her, his back to me now, his head going around and around and the room turning with it. My stomach revolted.

I bolted from the couch, stumbled past them into the bathroom and retched over the toilet. My whole head was numb now. The same thing had happened when my dog Laddie got hit by a car. My mother had demanded a response of grief from me. "Cry," she said and they all stood waiting, my sisters and my mother, waiting for me to cry. "You loved that dog," she said, "why don't you cry?" And I would not cry because I knew that she did not say it out of a feeling for me, but out of the necessity to be proven right, so she could say, "I told you, the world's a dirty place." My refusal to cry had cut its mark into me. And here I was, my grandfather had died and I was a piece of wood, numb in the head, unable to express what I should be feeling for an old man who had really cared about me.

"For God's sake," Claudette said. "Vomit and get it over with."

I tried, I strained.

"Shove your finger down your throat."

I stuck my finger into my throat, gagged, but nothing happened.

"Let me help," Claudette said. She stood behind me, wrapped her arms around my stomach and squeezed suddenly and hard. The flood of vomit, everything I had eaten, drank, whooshed forth, splattering the toilet seat. Once I began, I couldn't stop. I heaved and upchucked until there was nothing to come but green bile.

Claudette brought me water to drink, slapped me on my back as though I had just achieved something great. "Way to go," she said. "You'll feel better now. Whenever I drink too much, I just stick my finger down my throat and then I can keep on going."

"I'm not keeping on going," I said. "I'm going home. My grandfather is dead."

"So?"

I put my head into Claudette's pom poms. My face began to fall apart, piece by piece. My mouth trembled and I couldn't make it stop. I began to weep. "An old man is an old man, right? It doesn't matter what nationality, they're all the same. He was old and he was mine and he died."

"Christ," Claudette said and pushed me away. "I hate sloppy drunks."

But I didn't mind. I didn't care what anyone would say.

Journey to the Lake

MAURICE was in the basement when Truda came home for the weekend and her call had jarred him from his deep reverie. He looked about like a person awaking from a dream. He stood in the centre of the laundry room with a .22 rifle in his hands. Quickly, he put the rifle back into the rack on the wall. The automatic washer clunked into gear and began its final spin cycle. "Hello," Truda called down the stairs, "anybody home?" Their first words, all of his children, upon entering the house had always been the question, "Anybody home?" What did they think? Were they worried that everyone had vanished?

"Down here," Maurice called. He picked up the basket of wet laundry and went up to meet her. He smiled at the sight of Truda's large chunky body filling the doorway at the top of the stairs. He saw in her grey eyes the affection she had for him, magnified several times by the thick lenses of her glasses. She was plain, this daughter. Nothing pretty about Truda, but good and solid. He was almost sorry that she wasn't going to marry Brian, sorry for Brian that he'd missed out on Truda.

"Fancy meeting you here," Maurice said. "If I'd known you were coming, I'd have baked a cake." He set the basket down, hugged her tightly.

"Working overtime, I see," Truda said.

"A woman's work is never done," Maurice said. "I'm doing a few chores for the old lady. She had to work late tonight. Big wedding tomorrow. Just let me get this here out on the line and I'll rustle up a bite to eat."

"It's okay," Truda said. She shed her knapsack and set it on the floor. "I ate before I got on the bus."

"Well, I had a good supper too," Maurice said and thumped his stomach. "But that don't stop me from eating again." He'd gained more weight, he could feel it in the pressure against his belt buckle. Standing for any length of time made his abdominal muscles ache. But what the hell, he told himself, if a man can't eat, may as well shoot himself.

"Sit yourself down," he said. "Make yourself homelier, I won't be long." And he went out into the back yard to hang clothes on the line.

The basket of clothing bounced against his stomach as he carried it through the garden to the back yard where the clotheslines were strung between two trees. He stumbled and wet laundry slid down from the top of the pile onto the dirt. He swore, picked it up and shook it. He set the basket of laundry down on the hull of his nearly finished boat. He was breathing heavily; the effort of carrying the basket up the stairs and across the yard made his heart-beat rise. He felt the lack of oxygen in his cramped calf muscles. His body had become awkward, did not respond the way it should. He dropped things, walked into walls, felt like a drunk man.

He leaned against the boat and rested until his breathing became even.

Night was falling in the garden. He heard the sound of the town coming alive for a Friday evening. He no longer felt the pull of the town, though. He preferred now to do his drinking alone. He closed his eyes to the dots and bright flashes of light that danced in the air in front of him and saw old Henry Roy, lying in the narrow cot in the hotel room that had been his home, flesh falling away from his bones slowly. He saw the picture of a man locked inside a body that had given out on him; a living death. He shuddered and opened his eyes. What would be worse? He pulled the trigger and felt the hot path of metal through the roof of his mouth. The choice was his.

"What time do you think Mom will be home?" Truda asked.

"Eh?"

"Here, let me," Truda said and took the basket of laundry from him.

He felt foolish. She'd found him standing with his mouth open, staring into the neighbouring yard. He was aware of her hard look and conscious of his stomach, a ripe pumpkin straining the buttons on his shirt. His hair was still thick and black, but he was getting old. He talked to himself, for instance, aloud. He blurted out parts of sentences in French, inexplicably, to no one in particular. "*Je ne sais pas...*," he often said. He was unsettled by this because he had always thought he knew what was necessary to know.

Truda flicked a towel and hung it on the line. "I picked up the papers for you," she said. "I thought we might get started on them tonight."

Papers. What papers? "Oh, I see."

"You managed to get a copy of your birth certificate then?"

"Ah, what papers might that be?"

She turned and looked at him, a frown creasing the skin above her nose. "Your application for the old age security. We talked about it last weekend. Mom told me to pick the papers up for you."

He was irritated, first that he'd forgotten and then at Mika, for taking care of his business. "What did she want to go and do that for?" he asked. "It's a waste of time. I don't need old age security. I got security, I've got my work."

"What about after, when you can't work?"

He'd never allowed himself to think seriously about that. He knew he would have to quit eventually in some far-off time. He'd spend his days fishing, golfing or reading, although he did none of those things presently.

"I'll die with my boots on," he said. "They'll carry me out of the shop, feet first. Then I'll be pushing up the daisies. I don't need security." He saw old man Roy's eyes, the terrible lucidity in them, a fly crawling across an unshaven cheek, a hand frozen against a blanket, the short-circuiting of the brain freezing his body.

Two hundred and thirty-five pounds, the doctor whistled. Cholesterol count out of sight. What are you going to do about it? What happened to the diet? With proper drugs and weight loss, you never know. What would you do? Maurice asked. If you were me? The doctor walked away from the examining table. If I were in the shape you're in, I think I'd kill myself.

"You're going to be sixty-five this year," Truda said. "You're entitled to the pension."

"Let them give it to those that need it." Sometimes he felt as though he was building a monument.

"You've paid taxes all these years, why shouldn't you collect now? Look at it as being a kind of a refund."

A refund for living? Money given back to you, just before you died, as a kind of reward? Maurice sensed Truda's frustration and he softened. He realized that it was her attempt to look after him, provide for him. There was a time when he'd thought Truda was more flawed than the other children, the way she had stayed behind after they'd scattered and gone their separate ways. He knew her deep fear of being alone. "I guess that's one way of looking at it," he said. "I could just bank it, save it for my old age." He laughed.

"Lord," she said. "Use it to finish this boat. Hanging clothes around this beast is not the easiest. No wonder Mom complains. Do you think it'll be finished soon?"

The others had all stopped asking that question; even Mika had more or less resigned herself to the idea that he might never finish it, that the boat, overturned on two saw horses at the back of the yard, would become a permanent fixture. He wished Truda would stop asking as well. He ran his hand down the spine of the craft. "By cracky," he said. "All it needs now is the last gel coat and it'll be finished. Put an Evinrude on back of this baby and you won't catch me this summer, no siree. It'll be finished by the centennial celebrations."

He waited until Truda had finished hanging the clothes and they went back into the house. Truda set her knapsack on the kitchen table and took out a bottle of whiskey. Maurice was surprised. Truda drank?

"Do you mind?" she asked.

"Not so long as you pour one for me too," he said, and got two jelly jars down from the cupboard. Mika's shelves were lined with expensive glassware but Maurice still preferred the heavy squat shape of the jelly jar. He tried to be casual. He sensed that something was wrong. He'd been aware of all his children's problems coming inevitably in one shape or another over the years, and never without feeling guilty, of somehow being responsible. Because of this, he had never interfered with what Mika did when it came to the children.

Truda poured the drinks and Maurice made two thick corned beef sandwiches. Despite having eaten a large meal, he found that he had an appetite. He began to fill Truda in on the latest family news, retelling events he'd told her last weekend. And then something new, as though he'd only just remembered.

"They're going to change the name of this street. The street we live on. For the town's hundredth anniversary. What do you think it'll be?"

"Let me guess," Truda said. "They're going to name the street Rue Montreal, or Diefenbaker Place."

"Lafreniere," Maurice said. He swilled the rye about in his glass before tipping it up and finishing it. The heat of it in his stomach felt good.

"Well, hey, that's great. Can you believe it?"

"I haven't told your mother yet," Maurice said. "It's no big deal." He saw the moisture in Truda's eyes.

"When did this all come about?"

"At Christmas. Just before, I think. They told me their plans."

"I think it's a big deal. Imagine, Lafreniere Street after my old man."

"Not exactly after me," Maurice said. He poured himself another drink. "According to the history of this place, a Lafreniere was one of three names on the original incorporation of Agassiz as a town. They looked it up. It's in the records. But shoot, I don't mind. I'll take what I can get. Lafreniere's a good name." He chuckled softly. His father had no relatives; at least that's what he'd been told all those years when they'd lived as a family in the house, no, don't call it a house. It was more like a shack.

"*Je ne sais pas,*" Maurice said. Whether any of this matters or not. But pictures from his past kept rearing up and he was compelled to look at them against his will and there he was again, only thirteen years old, walking through the bush, stopping to look at a pocket watch.

Seven o'clock. It didn't matter. All he had was time. Soon he'd be swaddled in a damp blanket of cool air and, coming with nightfall, a chilling frost and he had nowhere to sleep, not yet. He'd raided the house once again for warmer clothing. There were weeds pushing through the cracks in the shack behind the house and he thought of his parents in the cemetery, only three weeks and already the weeds were growing upon their mounds of earth. He found nothing left behind in the house. It had all been taken. The windows were broken, not even the smell of his family remained, just the overpowering smell of wood rotting. But in the rafters of the shack was his father's .22 and a box of shells wrapped in heavy wax paper. He cut away from the house knowing he would never go back to it. He walked unseeing, a sleepwalker adrift in the real world. Heard a voice again today, he told himself, recording as in a journal. *It was like I was being followed; it was like a hand reaching to touch me.* He stopped, looked over his shoulder. Nothing but the leaves flipping gently, their thousand different autumn colours in the waning light. He blew his nose between his fingers. His hands smelled smokey to him, like the smell of a wild rabbit he'd snared that day.

Maurice sat staring, unblinking, into the jelly jar. Truda sloshed more whiskey into it.

"Cheers," she said and lifted her glass.

"Here's mud in your eyes."

"Okay, so when does this happen?" Truda asked. "When does this glorious name change take place?"

"Next month, during the homecoming. They're planning to have a boat regatta and a street dance."

"That only gives you a month to finish the boat," Truda said.

"It'll be ready. Old Man River is going to show those buggers what a boat really is. Take me a ride to the lake and back."

There was the sound of tires on gravel as Mika arrived home from work. They both gulped the remainder of their drinks and then laughed self-consciously over the fact that Mika still had this effect on them so that even now they felt guilty, had the urge to hide things rather than confront her. Maurice put the bottle into the cupboard.

Mika entered the kitchen carrying several packages. "Oh, you did come out," Mika said when she saw Truda. "Good, I've brought enough chicken and chips for three."

Maurice saw Truda about to protest and winked at her. "You don't say, chicken," he said. "That'll sure hit the old spot."

Mika unpacked the boxes of chicken and chips and set plates on the table. She switched the radio on and sat down to eat with them. Gospel music filled the room.

> I come to the garden alone,
> While the dew is still on the roses,
> And the voice I hear, falling on my ear,
> The Son of God discloses,
> And He walks with me...

The intimacy Maurice had felt changed instantly to something heavy and thick.

"I was hoping you'd make it out," Mika said. "I sure could use a hand. Roxanne Penner is getting married tomorrow, four bridesmaids' bouquets to be put together before two. Heard from Brian these days?" she asked Truda.

Maurice saw the blood rise in Truda's cheeks. She'd broken the news several weeks ago. Truda had decided to go to university instead of Flin Flon where Brian had been transferred as branch manager of a bank.

Mika chewed at a chicken wing. "I still don't think he'll wait four years," she said.

"I don't expect him to."

Mika pushed her plate aside. "What are you saying now?" she asked. "That you've changed your mind?" She reached for Truda's hand. "Where's your ring?"

"I've decided that I can't do both. I can't live in Flin Flon and go to university at the same time."

"That's ridiculous," Mika said. "You have to get married. You've practically lived with him for a year. I had to get married and so you have to, too."

Maurice was astonished at Mika's remark. Their eyes met. Mika leapt up from the table and began filling the sink with water. "What I meant to say was, we can't always do what we want," she said. "If your Dad and I had always done what we wanted, where would we be now?"

Far away, Maurice thought. With a bow ploughing the waves clean through. Out of the twisting shallow river into the clearer blue waters of the giant lake. The desire to do this had been strong, a ballooning pocket on the mainstream of his life. But, what will be, will be, he'd often told himself. It kept him from making decisions. He took what came.

> *...and He talks with me*
> *and he tells me I am his own,*
> *and the voice I hear falling on my ear,*
> *none other, has ever known.*

The women's voices and the nasal tones of the gospel singers grated, like stone against stone. He'd like to pull the plug and stop that damned depressing poor excuse for music.

"Education is fine and good," Mika said, "but small comfort on a cold night."

Maurice saw defiance coupled with fear in Truda's face. He got up and turned the radio down so low that the music was hardly audible.

"Mind your own business," Maurice said. "Can't you see the girl's made up her mind?"

Mika's jaw dropped. Maurice reached around her, took out the whiskey and plunked it down in the middle of the table. "Want a shot?" he asked Truda. She shook her head.

"Now, isn't that a thing for a father to say in front of his child," Mika said.

"To thine own self be true," Maurice said. "Look, what we say is neither here nor there," he said to Truda. "You know going to art school is what you want, what you can do, so go and do it."

"It's not art school," Truda said. "Fine Arts."

"Whatever." He poured whiskey into his glass. His hand shook.

Mika unbuttoned her suit jacket. She slipped it over the back of her chair. "That's a selfish way of thinking," she said. "You going to stay up all night?" she asked, not giving him the opportunity to defend himself. She looked pointedly at his glass of whiskey.

"As long as I want to," he said.

"Well, that would be nice," Mika said. "But I've got to get up early if I'm going to get that wedding done on time." She left the room.

"She was up at five this morning," Maurice said. "She works hard." He toyed with his glass, breathed deeply, fighting off depression. He was aware of Truda watching him too closely. "Let's get some real music going here," he said, forcing himself to sound jovial. "It's Friday night, after all. What we need in this here house is some toe-tapping music."

He went into the living room. The floor seemed to tilt beneath his feet and he stumbled against a chair. He put on a Don Messer record. "Now that's more like it," he said and yanked gently on Truda's hair as he passed by her chair. She had slumped down into it, and played with her glass in a listless way, as though she was tired, had no energy.

"Oh, I don't know," Truda said.

"What don't you know?"

"What we'd, what I'd ever do if you weren't here. This place…it wouldn't be…." She couldn't finish.

He was touched and pleased. "You'd go on, same as everyone else. But where would I be going? Shoot, I may get the boat in the river, but that's about all."

Truda reached for her knapsack, undid the buckles and withdrew a ceramic plate and two clay figures and set them on the table in front of him. "What do you think of these?" she asked.

"Where did you get them?"

"I made them."

"You don't say?" Maurice fingered the clay models. He picked one up. It was the figure of a small child, a young girl carrying a basket, crudely done, but the head and features looked realistic enough. "This looks like the real McCoy," he said.

Truda held up the plate. A bird divided the plate in half with its wing span, one side green, the other blue, the bird stark white. "You couldn't tell the difference between that and one in a store," Maurice said. "This art school, do you think you'll make much money when you're finished?" He didn't think many people would want the things she made, even if she could make enough of them.

"I'm having second thoughts," Truda said. "It was an idea. The instructor seemed to think I had talent."

"Sure you do. It's plain to see," Maurice said.

"But maybe Brian is right. I could pursue pottery as a hobby. He said he'd buy a kiln."

"What do you want to do?" Maurice asked.

Truda played with a honey-coloured braid that was draped across her shoulder and hung in a thick rope across her breast. She grinned sheepishly. "Both."

"But you can't do both."

"I know. I have to make a decision. God, I hate making decisions," Truda said loudly, stretching suddenly, and then she got up from the table.

"Let's get to work." She spread papers out on the table.

"What have you got there?"

"The forms. You know, for the old age security?"

He was confused. He couldn't remember what it was they'd said out by the clothesline. Something about a birth certificate. "Old age security. And what does that secure for me? Old age?" He was not going to fill in any bloody forms.

"A monthly income," she said. "So that you can retire."

"I'm not ready to retire."

She sighed. "Well I am. If Mom wants me to help with that wedding tomorrow, I'd better retire *tout de suite*. We'll work on this tomorrow."

Maurice cleaned the table off, set their glasses into the sink. He switched the light off and stood for a moment at the kitchen window, looking out at the garden and the dark shape of his unfinished boat. It would never float. Put an Evinrude on back of that baby and she would sink to the muddy bottom. He hadn't interpreted the instructions right. The diagrams hadn't shown how many layers of cloth or coatings of resin to apply. But even if he'd been able to understand, the boat wouldn't have been a success. He wasn't a builder. The kitchen window he'd installed was crooked. All through the house where his hand had been, doors did not close properly, carpet was set down askew, walls didn't line up. He was a failure.

He turned from the window and went into the basement to take the last load of clothes from the washer. The house was still. Above him he could hear Truda in the faint cracking of floorboards as she prepared for bed. He set the basket down at the foot of the stairs. He took the rifle down from its rack and sat down on the stairs with the gun across his knees. He shouldn't have said that, Maurice told himself, thinking of the doctor's words. That was not professional. He shouldn't have said that. And then he thought that he should write it down, the words the doctor had said in his office, so that they would know it hadn't been his idea entirely. He set the rifle aside, searched through his shirt pocket for a pencil. In the furnace room was a box of things kept for the visiting grandchildren, chalk and a chalk board. He took down a half-bottle of scotch from the top shelf, uncapped it and drank deeply. He found the chalk, went back to sit on the stairs.

He felt lightheaded. When he lifted his hand to write, he saw two hands. I, Maurice Ovide Lafreniere…he would write his statement on the wall. When he thought of Henry Roy and his full year of dying, he knew what he should do. To thine own self be true. Take his own good advice. I, he willed his fingers to write, but they wouldn't do as he wanted. Instead, he saw a jagged thick vertical chalk line on the cement wall. The chalk snapped. Truda was home. She would still be awake, hear the noise of the gun. He didn't want her to be the one to find him.

He lay beside Mika in bed. No moonlight shone in the window and it was totally dark in the room. He lay looking up at the ceiling, seeing nothing. To thine own self be true. Who had said that? Phrases, sentences, words that he'd picked out of the air all these years, formed by others. He had used them over and over without really knowing in what context they'd been said. He'd used words to build an image, not to express himself. Well, it's too late to start now, he told himself. To be, or not to be? To sail a boat, or not to sail a boat? No sail. Put an Evinrude on back of that baby and you won't catch me this summer. He closed his eyes, opened them again. He sensed that hand reaching to touch him lightly between the shoulder blades. He tried to find some shape to the room in the darkness. He had always been one to stalk a noise down in the night and call to it, who's there? Who's there? Through the window and pressed against the sky, he saw the bent shapes of branches reaching in the violet sky and he felt locked behind the window pane, looking out, unable to move, feeling a hand about to touch him in the centre, near his heart.

His breath quickened and heat spread across his body. Oh God, he said, and Holy Mother, Jesus Christ. He began to run. He ran along a worn path, familiar to him, running running. He caught sight of something buff-coloured off to one side of the path. He stopped dead, caught it up to himself knowing instantly what it was. It was his mother's moccasin, red beads, torn, bedraggled, pitched out of the house by unfeeling people. He clutched it to his breast and his grief rose in his throat. The smell of the soft leather was like his hands, like the smell of wild rabbit. Suddenly, a pinpointing of light pierced his head, a camera shutter opening and closing, and the bubble of his desire broke free and floated out into mainstream. Tears ran down the sides of his face into the pillow.

"Mika." He felt her beside him, warm. He willed his leg to move into hers, to wake her. It was pinned to the bed. He was wrapped tightly by fear, unable to move. He began to fight against it. Move, he instructed his arm and struggled to lift it off his chest. Sweat ran down his forehead. He felt the presence of something, someone standing beside the bed watching his struggle, waiting for him to give up. Move, he told his legs and strained against the blankets. He saw the soft glow of light in the hallway as Truda opened and closed her bedroom door.

"Truda." He heard footsteps going down the stairs. He fought to raise his head. His tongue was locked in his head.

"Maurice Ovide Lafreniere, is that you, or isn't that you?"

"It's me," Maurice said. Twigs snapped. He turned. It was his uncle, Old Man Desmarais.

"I've been looking all over for you," the old man said.

"Is it you then, who's been following me?"

Desmarais swept the navy toque from his head, spit into the bush. "You're a hard one to track." he said.

"What do you want?"

"I've come to take you to your people."

At last. Maurice felt the wind inside him die. His heart grew calm, slow. He clasped the old man's shoulders.

"Father, Father," Truda called. "Can you hear me?"

There were sounds about his head, a swarm of mosquitoes, humming. He slapped at them.

"Mr. Lafreniere, can you hear us?"

He should tell Truda, don't worry, you won't be alone. Do what you need to do. "Go away," he said in French. "I want to go home."

"What is he saying?" Mika cried.

Maurice felt the break coming. He felt the heavy earth slide downward as the dike gave way. "How will we get there?"

"Water, of course," the old man said.

"Of course. The river."

The canoe was waiting. Maurice stepped down into it, felt it rock gently. He knelt in the bow facing the river and picked up the paddle.

"You must speak English." Mika said. "We can't understand you."

"Father," Truda cried. "Oh Brian, he's slipping away. I can feel it."

The canoe rocked sharply as Desmarais pushed off and they floated out from the shadows into the dazzling light of sun on water. Maurice dipped the paddle and pulled gently. They moved forward silently. Behind him, he heard a harsh cry. It was the call of the blue herons. He turned and saw them, hundreds, rising from the water, necks pulled in tightly, iridescent beads dropping from their blue wings. Maurice felt the air moving as hundreds of wings fanned.

"Grab hold," Desmarais said. Maurice dropped his paddle. He saw it slipping away in the water and thought to reach for it. He would turn around, speak to them all one last time.

"No, no," Desmarais said. "We'll lose the birds. Grab hold quickly."

"But I—" I didn't fill in the forms.

"Now."

Now. Maurice reached, caught hold of a scaly, rough bird leg. Blue wings fanned about his head, struggled against his weight. He felt the bird's mighty strength in his hands. It faltered, climbed, and then he was skimming across the top of the water, weightless, free, upstream on the river, through its loops and curls out, out to the broad mouth where the colour of the water beneath him changed and the muddy silt settled to the bottom and there stretched before him the endless blue of the giant lake.

There is No Shoreline

A NAME in a newspaper. Menace to Society. Betty has been kneeling on the floor in the youngest child's bedroom, wrapping onion soup bowls and earthenware mugs into newspaper and placing them into a large trunk that sits on the braided oval mat in the centre of the upstairs bedroom. The items are new. They are surprises to be discovered when the youngest unpacks. It's a tradition. All her children expected, looked for the surprises. There are many shipping labels on the trunk. Labels of places she has only read about in newspapers or in the meagre pleading letters she's received from each travelling child. She reads the newspaper. Menace to Society. It's the name the judge has bestowed upon a man. It's like an axe splitting wood, she thinks, and is curious. Her long pale fingers unwrap the paper carefully, iron it flat against the rug. It seems that she gets all of her news this way, down on the

floor as she is slipping a sheet of newspaper beneath the cat's
dish or lining the bottom of a boot tray, or else when she is
packing or unpacking the paraphernalia that her four grown
children have acquired and carted in and back out of the house
on their many excursions into adulthood. It seems, too, that
the news she reads on the floor among the bits of dried cat
food or muddied shoes is more surprising, more interesting.
Menace to Society. Then she reads the man's real name. It
catches, like a hook meeting an eye, bringing two pieces of
fabric together. She has that kind of memory. She thinks that
it's compensation for her lack of travel, her inability to go
forward, this instant recalling of the past. It's a trick that she
doesn't understand or even want. She can be walking through
a crowded store or driving home from the supermarket and a
smell or a sound or a name read in a newspaper will suddenly
put her back inside a time. And she can reach out and touch
the sides of that time, hear the voices of it, the music, she can
smell the air.

She is behind the counter in the drugstore, refilling the
slots with cigarettes and feeling the blister on her heel brought
about by a pair of new red shoes. She silently curses her friend,
Del, for persuading her to spend the money on them. The bell
above the door jangles. She turns. A man approaches the
counter and scans the cigarette slots. Smoke from his cigarette
curls up into his heavy locks of blonde hair. It appears as
though his hair has been shellacked into place into a studied
careless arrangement across his forehead. He wears the type
of white T-shirt that her father wears beneath his barbering
shirts, but that men are beginning to wear now with blue jeans.
   "Players Plain."
   She slides the package from its slot and hands it to him.
His knuckles are cracked and rough-looking with black grease

imbedded in the chapped skin. A mechanic. His hands are like Frank's hands. I could never let hands like that make love to me, she tells herself. She wouldn't be able to stomach the smell of waterless hand cleaner or oily rags, or the smell of heavily greased hair on the pillow beside her. If she did, it would be against her will. She has vowed: never again, against her will.

The man rolls the change across the counter and then goes over to the payphone, walking with a slightly bow-legged swagger. Betty kneels, slides open the counter door and begins to rearrange the giftware inside. Two pale eyes meet her own through the glass casing. A child's mouth, pressed against the glass, resembles a snail climbing up the inside of a jar. Saliva dribbles down the showcase. Except for the pale eyes, the child is an exact replica of the man.

"Hey, come on, I've just cleaned that," Betty says.

His eyes shift sideways towards the man at the payphone, looking for protection, but the tongue remains on the glass.

Bribe him. She takes a two-penny sucker from the can on top of the counter, comes around the showcase and holds it out before him. His mouth pops loose from the glass, a grubby hand snakes forward and the sucker is gone. He wears a faded Mickey Mouse T-shirt, overalls which button at the legs and crotch, but the buttons have pulled loose and the overalls hang open like a skirt, exposing his ballooning plastic pants beneath. He scratches at his arms. Betty notices the bites on his arms. Some are the size of nickels, others of pimples.

She turns from the sight quickly. She doesn't need to feel sorry for him. So she goes over to the coffee bar instead and slips off the offending red shoes and feels sorry for herself. They cost twenty-five dollars. She has two jobs now. During the day she works as a filing clerk in the basement of the city hospital, next to the room where they conduct post mortems on corpses. Evenings and Saturdays she continues to work at the drugstore. She's sorry she purchased the shoes because she means to save every penny she can. It's important for survival. She wants to move out, away from this city, away from her past and from Frank, who has given up on his dream to become a country western singer and is now a machinist for a bus manufacturing company. This thick-lipped and heavy-lidded Frank who looks slightly Mexican is filled with excruciating desire to screw and make a family.

The child follows Betty to the coffee bar. He stares at her stocking feet. Just then, Rose, a middle-aged woman who runs the coffee bar, comes up from the basement, red-faced and puffing slightly from the stairs. "Well, well," she says. "Look who's here. If it isn't Mickey Mouse."

The child pulls the sucker from his mouth and replies indignantly, "Me Rocky, not Mickey Mouse."

"I should have known. You have big muscles. No wonder they call you Rocky."

The child's father hangs up the receiver. He swaggers over to the child and scoops him up awkwardly against his chest. "He's called Rocky after Rock Hudson.".

Rose ploughs forward the way fat people think they're entitled to. "I should have known. He's a handsome little devil. Just like his dad. I'll bet his mom spoils him rotten."

"He doesn't have a mother."

"Oh." Rose's expression is one of instant extreme concern. It makes Betty uncomfortable. Rose glances at the child quickly, leans across the counter and whispers dramatically, "What happened?"

The man meets her halfway across the counter. A smile forms on his blunt features. "She left me for a Harley-Davidson. What are you doing after work? I need a babysitter."

"Comedian," Rose says when the door closes behind them. She has offered concern and been scorned. "I'd of left him too. And did you see that kid? He was crawling with Lord knows what. I've never seen a kid so dirty. If there was one thing about my own, they were always clean. Not dressed in the best, but clean. There's no excuse for dirty."

Rose wears green or navy stretch pants with elastic waistbands to accommodate her fluctuating size, and loose flowered blouses to hide her pot belly. She smells of underarm deodorant. Betty doesn't mind that Rose takes pride in being ordinary, a carbon copy of most of the middle-aged women in the neighbourhood. But what she minds is that Rose lacks imagination. And people without an imagination can't see beyond their own experiences. She has not made the error of confiding in Rose.

Betty thinks that women talking about their children all sound the same. She goes back to the cigarette counter. She is anxious to arrange her counters, wipe the casing once again, count up the cash and be gone. She's to meet Del and the two of them will go to a travel agent's office to look at travel brochures. Betty doesn't know where she's going to travel to. She just knows she's leaving. Del, whose parents are in the armed services and who has lived all over the world, has the knowledge she needs. She leaves the drugstore. Her destination is a small park that fronts on Portage Avenue.

The day she began going to the park, Rose had been angry with her. "Why start hanging around that place?" Rose had asked. "What's the big attraction?"

Betty couldn't explain that Rose's company was beginning to make her feel claustrophobic. "It's outside, that's the big attraction. And I'm only going to eat lunch there; in my books, that's not hanging around."

"I can think of better places," Rose said. "You never know what could happen."

Betty was weary, anxious to have something happen. City people exaggerated. Betty doubted that there was real violence in the park because when she sat out on the veranda at night smoking a last cigarette, she listened to the kids who hung out there. Theirs was a phony bravado. They made her smile, they were so innocent.

"You sound like my mother," Betty said, knowing how to appease Rose. To Rose, life was a series of jobs that had to be done and Betty was one of those jobs. Even the recent adjustment to widowhood had been a chore Rose had tackled with determination. Rose had convinced Mr. Garvey to hire Betty, Against His Better Judgement. Experience had shown him that teen-aged girls were unreliable, he said. They never worked as hard as they could and left shortly after the first pay check or steady boyfriend. But even though Betty had proven otherwise, Rose still worried that any deviation from the established routine might be an indication that Betty was slipping and going the way of all the young woman that they had hired and then Mr. Garvey would be able to say, I told you so.

Rose dropped a sandwich and coffee into a paper bag with the same resolute efficiency with which she ran the coffee bar in Garvey's Drugs. "Listen here," Rose said. "I know what I'm talking about. Don't forget, there was a stabbing in that park only last weekend."

"A stabbing, hah. Someone cut their hand. The newspaper said it was self-inflicted, a game of some kind."

"Some game. They called an ambulance, you call that a game? I'll bet the city picked up the tab too. Let them bleed, I say. Play with matches, expect to get burned."

"Just like Home Sweet Home." Betty took the bag from Rose. "Look at it this way, I'm giving you something real to worry about for a whole hour."

"Get out of my sight," Rose said. "As if I haven't got enough."

Despite Rose's anger, she went to the park. She entered the quiet greenness and immediately it was cooler. There was a large rock garden in the centre of the park with castor bean plants in the middle of it. Her mother had attempted a rock garden once, but her mother was impulsive and hadn't thought it through first or planned it because she'd arranged the garden beneath a tree and nothing would grow in the shade. Gravel paths wound through the park from the four entrances and came together in the rock garden. Betty wiped dust from the bench before she sat down. She faced Arlington Street, the street where she lived. The sun tilted slightly in the west and made the houses on the street look more distinct. The houses had sharp edges, black shutters against white siding. Geraniums in windowboxes, motionless in the heat, were red splashes against the white houses. The house where she'd lived the past five months had an enormous graceful veranda which sloped down over her window in the front of the house like a grey umbrella. She realized with a start that the house was an attractive one, probably one of the nicer houses on the street. When she walked across that shiny, grey-painted veranda, passed between the white fake pillars and descended the wide jute-carpeted stairs, she saw her surroundings as though they were part of a photograph, a picture in a magazine.

Nothing seemed real to her. I am getting up and going to work, she recited. When she walked the two blocks to the drugstore, she counted the number of steps it took to get there. I am going home from work, she recited. She took her dinner from the oven where it was kept warm for her and ate it in her room. She was the only woman boarder. She heard the voices of the other boarders in the dining room as they played their daily cribbage games with the landlord. They talked about baseball scores and women. Or else she sat on her bed with her hands in her lap and watched the kids who ruled the park. They were her age. They wrestled each other to the ground and spat at people who walked by on the sidewalk. When she went to bed in the room at the front of the house beneath the grey veranda roof, she sometimes heard scrapings against the side of the house and saw shadows at the window. Or she heard water running in the toilet upstairs when someone forgot to jiggle the handle. She heard occasionally the sound of glass breaking in the night or a leather strap meeting flesh when the landlord pounded sense into the landlady. Nothing about the last five months seemed real to Betty. But she was beginning to wake up and her desire to get out and away from the drugstore was indication of it.

There was the crunch of wheels against the gravel path. A woman came around the rock garden pushing a stroller with a small child in it. She hesitated for a moment, framed by the tall red brick building which dominated the skyline behind her. When she saw Betty on the bench, she started towards her. The baby was fat and wore just a diaper and plastic pants. He leaned back into the stroller and looked dazed by the heat, asleep with his eyes open. As they grew closer, he looked at Betty, but without expression, as though she were part of the bench.

The feeling that made Betty want to eat lunch in the park also made her want to try to make something happen in the baby's face. She leaned towards the child and smiled. The baby's eyes flickered briefly and then he poked listlessly at the plastic balls attached to the front of the stroller. The woman came alongside Betty and stopped, interpreting the smile as an invitation to visit. She was tall and stringy. She wore a red elastic tank top that squashed her small breasts flat. Her legs and arms were tanned, but a puffy bulge of white stomach squeezed overtop her jean shorts.

"Sure is hot," the woman said.

"Hotter than yesterday," Betty said. She'd learned how to small talk from listening to Mr. Garvey and Rose over lunch, and the customers thought she was mature for seventeen because she could engage them in pleasant but meaningless chatter.

"And here it is, the end of August. You'd think we'd be getting some relief by now," the woman said.

"The forecast is for more of this tomorrow."

"Wouldn't you know it?" the woman said with a look of mock despair. "I'm in an apartment. Top floor and no air conditioning. Tigger's got the worst heat rash."

"Who?"

She laughed and motioned to the baby. "It's what we call him," she said. "His real name is Brian, but I don't think he knows it. We used to have a cat named Tigger." She pushed the stroller back and forth on the gravel path with short movements. The child's head jerked forward and backwards into the canvas stroller. Stupid broad, Betty said silently, feeling that careless motion, feeling sudden anger.

"It was a tabby cat. A grey tabby, you know the kind," the woman said. "They look like tigers? I really liked it. We had to take it with us when we went camping in the Whiteshell last year and it got away on me."

"That's too bad," Betty said. She was sorry that she'd smiled at the baby.

"It ran into the bush the first day we got there. You know what happened to it? It went wild," the woman said, not waiting for an answer. "Apparently cats do this. Dogs don't, but the camp warden said it happens all the time with cats. Then the wardens have to hunt the cats down in late fall and shoot them," she said with a certain smug satisfaction.

They use them for target practice, I'll bet, Betty told herself. "That's terrible."

"Oh, you don't need to feel sorry for them," the woman said. "They're wild and I mean wild. You can't come near them. It's a kindness really to shoot them because they'd just freeze to death when winter came. Anyway, I'm looking for another one. And when I saw you sitting here, I thought I'd come over and see if you might know of someone who's giving kittens away."

"No I don't, sorry."

"Tigger here needs a pet, don't you sweetie?" She squatted in front of the stroller and prodded the flaccid child in the chest in an attempt to make him smile.

Betty saw the skin on the inside of the woman's thighs as she squatted. It was darker, as though it was permanently stained. The insides of her own legs were not like that. Brown pubic hair curled outwards from the woman's denim shorts. Her tanned hand rested on the stroller and Betty saw that she wore a wide gold band. The woman was married then and could know who the baby's father was. More and more Betty wondered who the father of her own baby might be.

"Who was it?" Mika, Betty's mother, had asked. She wanted to know, hoping, Betty realized, to pressure them into marriage.

"I don't know," Betty said. It was true. She didn't know. It could have been the tall blue-eyed man, the one who was training to be an RCMP. She'd first seen him sitting in the vestibule of the hotel when she passed by the window. She knew what the men who sat there watching women pass by were like, the bets they made, the words they used: bitch, cunt, whore. But when the patrol car pulled alongside her one night and the young one laughingly threatened to arrest her for wearing a tight sweater, she laughed too, because they were in uniform and she disassociated them from the hotel men. They offered to give her a lift home and she accepted, anticipating with mild glee Mika's frantic reaction about what the neighbours would think when they saw her. But the men didn't take her straight home. They took her instead into the country to an abandoned farm house. The young one led her into the house and told her to lie down and then she understood. All she felt was anger at her own stupidity and saw this as the penalty to be paid for it. He entered her while the older man stood watch in the doorway. She saw the moon resting upon his shoulder

Sometimes when she was on a bus or sitting on the veranda smoking, she would think about this and cry out involuntarily. When people stared at her strangely she'd realize that she'd let the interior pass through to the exterior and had exclaimed loudly and so she would count to herself, the number of stairs in a building, the seconds it took for a light to change from red to green, to prevent it from happening. But more and more she was letting herself think and when she counted the days, months, she was certain that it had been the RCMP man who had gotten her pregnant.

"Well, if you do hear of someone who is giving away a kitten, could you let me know?" the woman said. "I'll give you my number."

"You can if you want to, but I don't know many people in the city. I'm new here."

"Oh, too bad, Tigger should have a pet. Shouldn't you Tigger, eh? What do you say?" She tickled his armpit fiercely. "Come on, what do you say?"

Betty saw his head wobble slightly on its thin stem-like neck. He squirmed. Then Betty saw his mouth crinkle, move into a wide smile that did not reach into his eyes. What choice did he have but to smile? The woman is stupid, she told herself.

"How old is he?" Betty asked.

"Thirteen months in October." The woman got up, brushed a strand of hair from her forehead and surveyed the park with dark nervous eyes. "I don't know what I'll do once he starts walking. What this park needs is a wading pool for the little kids. A playground. This place has become such a hangout."

"That's bullshit," Betty said. "Everyone says that, but I live right across from here and I've never had any trouble."

The woman turned the stroller around sharply and began to walk back in the direction that she'd come. "And I wonder why," she said over her shoulder. "I just wonder why."

Betty watched as the woman lifted the stroller from the gravel path onto the sidewalk. Behind them, the tall red brick building jutted up from among the houses conspicuously and Betty counted floors, the fifth, the window on the corner. That had been her room, where she'd spent the winter and spring behind the glass looking down at the streets. Her baby had been a boy too. He'd been a big child, a coke and chocolate bar baby, the nurse had said. She thought he'd break her pelvic bones when he came. It's like menstrual cramps, Mika had said as she bent over the bread pan, her fists working the dough throughout their conversation, only it's a hundred times worse.

"I'm sorry," Betty said. She watched as Mika's fist plunged into the swollen bread dough. It fizzled and sank. No calamity or illness interfered with Mika's work.

"You're sorry," Mika said. "Good." There was perspiration in the fine hair above her top lip. The cords in her neck were strung tightly. "But what will that change, tell me?" She took the knife, sliced the dough into two and then once again. She held up a piece of it and formed a loaf. "It's not a mass or a tumour, you know. If you cut it, it will bleed."

"What do you want me to do?"

"Give it up. It's the sensible thing to do." She plopped the loaf into the greased pan and began to form the second.

"But what if I want to keep it?"

"You? Keep it? What do you know about children?"

"What did you know?"

"Listen," Mika said. "It's going to hurt. Like menstrual cramps, only a hundred times worse; as it should. But if you keep the baby, the trouble only begins. Children are a constant pain." She wiped her eyes on her sleeve. She led Betty into the bedroom and gathered several limp cotton smocks from the back of the closet and pushed them down into a shopping bag in a furtive way as though they were shameful depressing items. "Be sensible. Don't ruin your life," she said. "Give it up."

"I don't know," Betty said.

"Well, do what you want, but don't bring it home to me," Mika said.

Mika had never used the word baby. So when the nurse placed the baby into the crook of Betty's arm, she was surprised at its warmth and heaviness and the soft curve of its reddish-blonde head beneath her hand.

The feeling that came to her, that had made her want to eat lunch in the park, vanished. The sandwich Rose had made tasted like cardboard. She got up from the bench, counted the number of strokes it took to brush crumbs from her lap. She felt as though she carried an egg around inside her. An egg with a crack in it, starting from the top and going down to the bottom. It would split open.

Betty meets Del in the park and the two young women walk down Arlington Street to Portage Avenue where they'll catch a bus downtown. The park has become the centre for their friendship. They go there often to sit and listen to the city. Occasionally, they talk with the boys who also gather there. And often, through a series of body movements, a secret language with one of the young men, Del sends messages, and like a tawny urgent cat, she sidles into the shaded back portion of the park to some boy's blanket. But not Betty. She has learned her lesson and nothing interferes with her goal to flee this city as soon as possible. The means to do this takes shape in the metal tea can in the bottom bureau drawer.

As they near Portage Avenue, Betty becomes aware of a car moving alongside them, slowly. She turns to look. It's the man from the drugstore and his scruffy child. He salutes the women in a showy manner, stops the car and rolls down the window.

"You girls look like you could use a lift. Going far?"

A thousand miles, Betty thinks.

"That depends," Del says. She flashes a golden dimpled smile. "He's cute," she whispers.

"Cute like a snake."

"Depends on what?" he asks.

"Who owns the kid?"

"He's mine, but I'm not married, if that's what's stopping you."

"What can go wrong with a kid along?" Del asks and they get into the car.

They drive around the city for two hours, a listless aimless way. His name is Dave Reimer, they learn. He is a single parent. He does not say to them, I am a single parent. He is reluctant, almost ashamed to speak about it at any length. She took off, is all he says. But Del has an easy way of talking about intimate or personal things that is not in keeping with the times and once people get over their initial shock, they respond to her. Dave tells her Rocky's mother left when he was a year old. With some guy on a motorcycle. The sympathy in Del's green eyes is innocent and genuine.

At the end of the two hours, Del has joined Dave in the front seat and Rocky has climbed over into the back seat and bounces on the seat beside Betty, showing no signs of being tired although it's ten o'clock. They cross the river several times. It seems to Betty that they've been driving in circles. When Dave crosses the river once again, this time it's over an older rusting bridge, and they enter what appears to be the old section of Winnipeg. The street they travel on ends in the river. The lights of city centre across the river bank are reflected back in the dark water. At the last moment, Dave swings the car to the right and they bump along a rutted dirt road. He turns off his headlights. Ahead, at the end of the road beside the dark still river, is a tall building. It looms up at them suddenly, white like the billowing sails of some ancient ship.

"Time to put the kid away," Dave says. He turns off the engine.

"Where are we?" Del is nervous, uncertain.

Dave motions to the tall building. "It's home. Rocky and me live here." It's an abandoned grain elevator.

They pass through the black slit of the sliding door and Dave pushes it closed. He switches on his flashlight. The circle of light flickers, barely dents the dark interior. The building smells dankly of urine, wood, gunny sacks and something else. Betty doesn't know what.

"Here." Dave guides them up a little step. The floor suddenly sways beneath their feet. Betty reaches wildly, finds a railing and hangs on. "It's just the lift," Dave says. Then she hears the squeal of metal, the squeaking protest of wood beneath her feet. Pulleys clank. The smell of rope is strong. She's being drawn upwards. The air grows warmer and smells faintly of straw. She still doesn't believe he lives here. The lift carries them up and up and then it stops.

"This is it," Dave says. He carries Rocky in his arms and shines the light for them. The light touches a small room. Betty catches sight of a rumpled bed and then clothing hanging on pegs. Dave sets Rocky down and squats. He strikes a match. It flickers and then a glow spreads outwards from the camper's lantern on the floor. He moves across planks that bow beneath his weight, kneels once again and another lantern sputters, hisses and spreads its light. Betty looks about the room. There's a narrow cot in one corner, a grey sleeping bag on the floor beside it. Nails hold clothing on the wall and the floor is spread with what looks and smells like dirty laundry. Dave shuffles through it, moves it from his path as he crosses the room. A cardboard box beside the cot is filled to overflowing with toys. On the other side of the room a large wooden spool is used as a table. She's seen the spools in the ditches along the highways. They hold hydro or telephone wire. The spool is scattered with pop and beer bottles, some paperback books and a carton of cookies.

Del stands transfixed. Then suddenly for some reason, she takes it upon herself to take charge of Rocky. She croons over him and pulls his Mickey Mouse T-shirt off over his head. "Look at his curly eyelashes. They're so long. Isn't he cute?"

Betty studies the child's face and wonders what it is she's missed. She feels nothing but impatience to be away from this place. She crosses the planks and goes over to Dave. He squats, adjusting the flame in the lantern. Her footsteps are suddenly hollow. Dave holds up the lantern. She sees the foot of black space on either side of the planks. Her skin crawls. "God."

Dave grins. "Isn't that something?" He searches behind him on the floor, holds up a pop bottle and then lets it drop into the black space. Seconds later, Betty hears the dull thud of it hitting the earthen floor below.

"That goes down into the grain bins. I keep boards over it all the time. There're ladders going down to the bottom, though. If I couldn't use the lift, I could climb down."

A grain elevator. In the centre of the city. The air is thick and stifling hot. "What about Rocky? Aren't you worried that he'll fall?"

"I thought of that," Dave says. He crosses back over the planks and gathers up Rocky, who is naked now except for his sagging plastic pants. Dave takes a leather harness down from a nail on the wall and slips Rocky's arms into the harness. He buckles it in the back. Rocky doesn't struggle or seem to mind. He carries Rocky to the bed and puts him into it. There's a rope lying on the floor, looped about the leg of the cot. He picks up the rope and snaps it to the fastener on the back of the harness.

"Houdini couldn't get out of that one." He reaches beneath the cot and pulls out a box of beer. He opens three and motions the way to them back across the planks. A tiny window is nailed

over with sacking at the far end of the room. Below the window
on the floor are cushions from a discarded couch. Dave motions
for them to sit down. Betty thinks of bugs and the bites on
Rocky's arms and is reluctant. But Del sits down immediately,
seeming not to notice the smell or the heat.

"Why don't you open a window? God, it's hot," Betty says.

Dave sits down beside Del. "Can't. The mosquitoes
are hell."

She's impatient to be gone. He's brought them both here
for a reason. She's anxious to get it over with. "Why do you
live here? It's a shitty place for a kid to live."

"I live here because I love it, right?"

"Come and sit down," Del says. "We didn't have anything
better to do anyway."

Betty does so reluctantly. Dave motions towards the child
who is sleeping, curled and asleep so suddenly. "Children's Aid
is looking for him. They want to put him into a foster home."

"How come?" Del asks.

"Because. They say I can't look after him properly. When
Rocky's mother took off, my mother babysat for me. But she's
working now herself. She can't do it anymore."

Betty can hear the wind. It has always been there, but as
she thinks about what he's just said, she becomes aware of the
wind in the rafters, swaying the whole building so that it cracks
and snaps above and below, all around them. It's as though they
are moving with it across some ocean in the middle of the
prairie. Grain elevators, the sailing ships of Lake Agassiz. The
idea intrigues her. Or, it's the ghostly sound of the carts, she
imagines, the historic freighters of the prairies that echoes in
the rafters of the elevators.

She hears another sound. It comes from beneath them.

"What's that?"

"Rodents."

"Rodents. You mean mice?"

"Rats."

"So. What do you do then?" Del asks quickly, seeming not to want to think: rats. She forms the question that Betty has wanted to form, has thrown away instead to the listening of the wind and imaginings.

"What can I do? I leave him here."

Betty gets up, showing disgust and impatience. "What can you do? Quit working. Collect unemployment insurance. Go on welfare. Something."

"Hah. Very funny. Think I haven't thought of that? They don't give men welfare so they can stay home with their kids."

Betty wants to reach up and tear the burlap from the tiny window, to feel the fresh air. Dave pushes past her. He gets another warm beer from the box beneath the cot and comes back to sit beside Del. He searches about in his hip pocket, slips a snapshot from his wallet. He holds it up to Betty first. It's a picture of a young girl who squints into the sun, holding a bundle of blankets in her arms. Betty sees herself in the picture. They have both abandoned their sons; the fate of her own child is less clear, perhaps he is the child of a mother who bangs his head against the stroller when walking gravel paths in the park. To a baby, what mother it has doesn't matter as long as someone feeds it and holds it close. It's later that it matters.

"We went steady for a year before she got pregnant."

Del refuses to look. "What does Rocky do? When you're at work, what does he do?"

"He sleeps most of the time. That's why I keep him up late. Then I come by and see him at noon. Change his diapers. The longest part is the afternoon. He's not tired then. It gets hot."

Del looks frightened. She stares at the sleeping child. "That's awful. I think that's the saddest thing I've ever heard."

"I just don't know what else to do. We won't be able to stay here in winter. We'll freeze," Dave says.

"Well, you're going to have to think of something," Betty says, making it clear that she thinks it's his problem.

"Are either one of you interested in babysitting for free?"

Del and Betty are silent. They don't speak of Rocky again and when the three of them leave, Betty hears the child breathing gently and sees the rising and falling of the grey sleeping bag against his chest. She feels stricken. As though she personally is abandoning him, setting him adrift in the bowels of the creaking ship, and there is no shoreline.

The following day, Del comes to work with Betty and sits at the coffee bar chatting with Rose whom she adores. Each time someone comes into the drugstore she turns to look and so when Dave and Rocky arrive, Betty isn't surprised. Del leaves the drugstore with them and Betty doesn't see them again until she's finished work and walks into her room. They are there, the three of them, wrestling on her bed.

Dave gets up immediately, swooping Rocky from Del's stomach where he has been bouncing against her knees. They are play-acting, Betty realizes. They are engrossed in each other's giggles and stupid horseplay. They think they're a happy family. As though a family is just that: play slaps and tickles to make one feel happy.

Dave and Rocky leave quickly. Del leans against the bureau looking guilty. "We had no place to go," she says.

Betty straightens the spread on the bed and hates herself for doing so. She's becoming old, tidy, like her mother. She is becoming what she is. "You might have asked."

"I will next time. Sorry."

Betty is irritated that they've seen her strewn clothing and begins to fold things. She pulls open her bottom drawer on the pretense of putting the clothing into it so that she can check the metal tea can without being conspicuous. It appears to be untouched. She will open an account in the bank. No sense taking chances with her future.

Del winds and unwinds a strand of golden hair that has pulled loose from her pony tail. "I'm moving in with Dave," she says with unaccustomed shyness.

"Congrats. Dave has his instant mother."

"So? So, what's wrong with that?"

"You want that? Don't you know that's what he's been looking for, for someone to come and be a free babysitter? Someone who will care for him and his kid?"

"He's no different than any other man," Del says. "It's just that the kid is born already. That's the only difference. Anyway, what's wrong with wanting to look after a man and kids?"

Nothing. Betty has to admit that. Nothing. Someone at this moment is looking after her own child. She wants to cry.

"We were wondering. All we need is a little money. Enough for the first month's rent and groceries. We could swing it then. Do you think you could?" Her gaze strays to the bottom drawer.

Betty freezes. "No bloody way. Forget it."

"It's okay. I have other options."

But Betty knows she doesn't.

The matter of the money becomes a point of tension between them. But even though Del sees Dave often, she still comes occasionally to talk to Betty. She sits with one leg slung over the railing of the veranda or in the park with her knees gathered to her chin, breaking smoke rings with her slender fingers. But their friendship is not the same. Betty has decided to move to Vancouver. She feels guilty though, for being the cause of the friction and so when Del comes over one evening and asks to borrow a sundress, she complies with too much eagerness, lavishing accessories unasked upon Del. She is inside, dressing when Dave comes to pick her up. Instead of waiting in the car as he usually does, he comes to the house and leans against the railing of the veranda where Betty sits on the steps. As though he's just remembered something important,

he pulls an envelope from his shirt pocket and hands it up
to Betty.

"It's Rocky's birthday card."

Betty opens it. Happy Birthday Rocky, written in a spread,
breathless sort of handwriting. There are x's and o's at the
bottom of it. Paper-kissed kid. Painless mothering, she thinks,
and then flinches slightly.

"I think it means something," he says, "don't you? I mean,
would she have bothered to send it if she didn't care?"

It didn't cost anything to agree. "Probably not," Betty
says and hands him back the card.

Rocky toots the car horn and Dave shakes his fist. "Kids,"
he says, as though she should know what it means to say, kids.

"I don't know," Dave says. "Sometimes I think that if she
saw him, she'd want to come back. It's the only reason I've kept
him. What do you think?"

Del comes across the veranda and the question goes
unanswered. She looks beautiful, her tanned shoulders framed
by the straps of the white sundress, her gold earhoops bobbing
as she walks, accentuating her square jaw. She sees Rocky in
the car and her wide smile vanishes.

"I thought you were getting a sitter?"

Dave shrugs, holds his hands up to indicate his helpless-
ness. "I tried but I just couldn't get anyone."

"But we've never been anywhere without him."

Betty wants to laugh. She wants to say, see? But then she
thinks of Frank. Frank who knows all about her and still
persists. This could be them, wanting to go out, needing a
babysitter. She feels guilty for wanting to laugh. "You wanted
to go out? I'll babysit Rocky," she says.

Dave drops them off at the elevator. Betty waits for him to
leave and then tears the burlap from the window. She holds
Rocky up to it. Together they watch a man peeing in the Red
River. Children, she supposes they're his, play at the river's

edge. They wave willow branches in the air, dip them into the water. She becomes heartsick suddenly; it's like a gush of salt water in the back of the throat, for her brothers and sisters.

"I've done the sensible thing," she'd said. "It's over. You can send Dad in to get me. I'm calling from a drugstore on Arlington Street."

"The sensible thing would have been not to get pregnant in the first place," Mika said. "Now what?"

"I could always go back to school." Rose was listening in, wiping the counter top carefully, staying in one spot too long. Betty turned her back to the counter.

"You wouldn't fit in. You'd be the butt of every joke."

"I could get a job."

"There aren't any jobs in Agassiz."

"What do you want me to do then?" Her sweater was damp, her breasts were oozing milk.

"The sensible thing to do would be to stay in the city and get yourself a job. Start over again. But you're welcome to come home on weekends, if you like."

The man zips up and continues to walk along the river bank. The children follow like birds lifting and swarming and settling back down over some muddied object left lying. Across the river, water sprinklers swish dust from the sidewalks and cool dark stains spread out beneath the trees. The odour of exhaust from the traffic is trapped by the thick foliage along the riverbank. Above the city, neon lights colour the sky pink. Betty has never felt violence in the streets of the city. But she knows that it's there. It's there in the houses and apartments on Arlington Street, where everything is carefully laid down behind clearly defined borders of picket fences and hedges and the panes of glass in the windows. She holds Rocky and makes another vow. Not in my house, she says, never in my house.

She rummages through the box of toys and finds a tattered *Golden Book.* She attempts to read to the child, but he keeps sliding from her lap, wants once again to be lifted to the window to watch the children play.

She blows up a beach ball and for a time he is happy. She waits for him to become tired and when his eyes grow heavy and his coordination sluggish, she's relieved.

She sits beneath the open window on the cushions in the gathering darkness and waits for Dave to return. She has the flashlight by her side should Rocky awaken. She listens to the sounds of the building. She feels the building sway. She puts her hands to its floor boards. She feels the vibration. Wood snaps. Overhead, rafters groan as dry wood rubs against dry wood. She imagines wind filling a canvas sail. Then the hair on her arms rises. The other sound. She reaches for the flashlight, flicks the switch with trembling fingers, sweeps the light across the floor in the direction of the scuffling sound. She sees the thick grey tail disappear into the shadows.

She leaps from the cushions. She shines the light across Rocky. There's another swift shadowy movement from beneath his bed towards her feet. She screams and kicks out at it. It swerves and scurries behind the cushions where she has been sitting.

Rocky begins to cry. He sits up in bed. He wraps both hands around the rope that holds him there. He rocks back and forth, his voice is a monotone wailing, an eerie chanting that she knows is not right for a child. The sound of it is worse than the sight of the rats. She pushes aside her own terror. She gathers the child to her. She places the flashlight on the cot to chase away the shadows and she sings to him lullabies that have sprung up from some deep underground stream.

The following day she gives all her money to Dave.

"Thanks," he says, "I'll never forget this."

The next day he is gone. He takes the money and Rocky and vanishes. Del waits several days and then joins her parents in Toronto. Betty never sees any of them again.

"What, not finished packing yet?"

It's a question put to Betty by the youngest child. The one she's packing for, the one she's played Brahms and Bach to and hung delicate-sounding chimes above the crib for; the youngest is leaving home. She stands on the braided oval mat with two large parcels clutched against her small breasts. Her questioning eyes are Frank's brown eyes, surprised, but good naturedly puzzled by her mother's dreaming. Frank calls Betty a rare bird and has given her what she's needed. All Betty had when she married Frank was the new red shoes. He makes jokes about that now.

Somewhere, a child grew up without me, she wishes to tell the youngest. He has as much to do with shaping your existence here as have the first settlers, the women who cranked out their years in a one-room sod house, the Indians who hunted these plains for buffalo, or the Mennonite farmers. But she won't say it. She will, instead, move the memory out across an ancient lake and leave it there to find its rest among the glaciers.